DINING WITH DISASTER...

The pretty Irish gal went to serve a couple of new customers. Longarm heard her ask, "What can we get for you boys this evening? Steaks are our specialty, but the Irish stew is mighty tasty and filling."

"I want a big bowl of chili," the larger of the pair demanded, his words angry and slurred from drinking. "I don't want no damned steak or stew. Chili."

"We don't have chili on the menu tonight," Milly explained. "How about some hash or ..."

"Gawdammit woman, are you deaf?" John shouted.

Longarm laid his knife and fork down and was just about to come to his feet when Rory burst out of the kitchen. "Get out of here!" he bellowed. "I don't need your business!"

The big man started to come out of his chair, bellowing, "Mister, you and this dumb bitch can go straight to hell!"

Rory punched the loudmouth on the side of the head, knocking him out of his chair. Then he turned to the other man at the table and shouted, "I said to get out ... both of you!"

"All right," the one named George agreed. "Just take it easy there. We're going."

Rory turned to Milly. "Never mind them. They're just liquored up and ignorant."

Suddenly John raised a pistol, took aim, and fired. Longarm had just started to pick up his knife and fork when the shot boomed out, and he saw Rory spin around, grabbing his shoulder. The shooter thumbed back the hammer of his six-gun, and would have shot Rory dead, but Milly hurled a glass of beer at John, sending his second shot into the ceiling. By then, Longarm was on his feet, knocking over his table and drawing his gun ...

TABOR EVANS

LONGARM

AND THE
SCORPION MURDERS

J

JOVE BOOKS, NEW YORK

LONGARM AND THE SCORPION MURDERS

A Jove Book / published by arrangement with
the author

PRINTING HISTORY
Jove edition / June 2001

The Penguin Putnam Inc. World Wide Web site address is
www.penguinputnam.com

ISBN: 0-515-13065-6

A JOVE BOOK®
Jove Books are published by The Berkley Publishing Group,
a division of Penguin Putnam Inc.,
375 Hudson Street, New York, New York 10014.
JOVE and the "J" design
are trademarks belonging to Penguin Putnam Inc.

PRINTED IN THE UNITED STATES OF AMERICA

10 9 8 7 6 5 4 3 2 1

Chapter 1

United States Marshal Billy Vail motioned Longarm into his office at the downtown Denver Federal Building. "Sit down, Custis. I appreciate you coming in like this on the first day you've had off in weeks."

"Months," Deputy Custis Long corrected. "Billy, I was going to spend the day in bed sleeping."

"What for? You'd still be going out on the town at night with some pretty gal. Spending your hard-earned wages. Having fun."

Longarm leaned back in the office chair and shook his head. "I don't know why you have to call me in when there are about a half-dozen other deputies poking around here in the Federal Building."

"Because that's about all they're any good for ... poking around. But you, now you're the one man that I can count on when I've got a tough case to assign."

Longarm shook his head. "I ain't going to fall for your flattery, Billy. And I'm not going to put off my vacation again. In fact, I've got a train ticket down to Santa Fe, New Mexico, and a pretty little *señorita* that I mean to have some fun with later this week."

"She'll wait for you," Billy said. He was short, non-

1

descript, middle-aged, and badly out of shape . . . going to fat actually. In contrast, Longarm was in his mid-thirties, stood six foot four, and was lean, hard, and handsome. Sometimes their size difference made Billy feel a bit inferior, but he was the senior officer, the manager who had once also been a field deputy marshal bringing in his share of outlaws in his prime. "Women love you, Custis. Being as how you're so ugly, I don't understand it, but they do."

"I don't know about that," Custis said, feeling uncomfortable talking about women because that was something he had been taught not to do when he was a boy growing up in West Virginia. "But you didn't ask me here to shoot the breeze about my love life. And I'm tellin' you straight out that I'm not going to cancel another vacation just because you don't trust someone else to handle the dirty work."

"Dirty work!" Billy protested. "When have I ever given you any dirty work?"

"Just about every assignment I get is one that no one else in this building would touch. Have you already forgot about how you sent me into Death Valley this *summer*?"

Billy shrugged. "That's not where I sent you. I sent you to the green and cool Sierra Nevada Mountains of California. How was I to know that the outlaws had their hideout in Death Valley?"

Longarm snorted with disgust. He'd damn near died of heat stroke in Death Valley and he still hadn't fully recovered from the ordeal.

"Custis, I have an assignment that is . . . well, it would mean a promotion for you."

Longarm scoffed. "You know damn good and well that I'm not interested in any promotion. I've seen what a desk job and the politics of managing a government office has done for you, Billy. I want no part of either."

"The assignment that I have for you is really important."

"You say that about all of them." Longarm had heard

2

enough. He climbed out of the chair with every intention of getting through the door and out of the building before his old friend talked him into doing something that he didn't want to do.

"I'm serious about this one, and it involves someone out of your past. Custis, it involves Jesse Jerome, your old friend and mentor."

Longarm stopped halfway to the door. He turned. "Did you say Jesse Jerome?"

"That's right."

"He was a fine good officer and teacher when I first signed on as a deputy marshal, but this department decided he lacked the necessary temperament."

"Jerome was the meanest, toughest, most devious, and most charming man I've ever known," Billy said. "He also happened to enjoy beating and killing people."

"Only those who deserved it," Longarm argued. "I rode with him for two years and he never once shot an innocent man."

Billy shook his head. "Let's not argue about Jerome. We both know that he considered himself judge, jury, and executioner. He never brought a man back alive if he could help it, and that's not the way that the law works. Guilty until proven innocent. We don't judge the guilt or innocence of people we arrest. We simply bring them in and allow the court to make that determination. Jesse Jerome never accepted that he was an officer of the law, not a damned bounty hunter."

"Look," Longarm said. "I'll admit that Jesse was a little hotheaded. Maybe a mite quick with his fists and his six-gun too. But he was fair. I saw him risk his life dozens of times trying to give the fella we was after the benefit of the doubt before killing him."

"Spare me!" Billy cried, throwing his hands up in the air. "Have you forgotten that Jerome actually hung four men in Montana? Now don't tell me that happened by accident."

3

"All killers, Billy. They killed three children, if you remember, and raped their mother before they bashed in her head. Last I heard, she never regained her good senses. If ever four men deserved to be hanged on the spot, it was those four."

"If you had been there, could you have stopped Jesse?" Billy demanded. "Or perhaps the better question is . . . would you even have tried?"

Longarm came back to the chair and sat down. "I've asked myself that same question a time or two, and I guess the answer is that I just don't know. I expect I'd probably have shot them instead of using a rope. Belly-shot them, that is."

"Don't ever do something like that, Custis. No matter how vile, how heinous the crime, never kill anyone when you can arrest and bring them in for trial. If we go around the court system and start becoming the final word on guilt or innocence, we're doomed."

Longarm shook his head. "Those four men that Jesse hanged had raped and killed before. He was weak and badly wounded, and they were too much for him to bring in given the situation. As hard and as tough as he was . . . those four would have found a way to kill him before he could get them to a jail."

Billy stood up and turned to his window. "Custis, I'm beginning to think," he said quietly, "you aren't the right man for this assignment. Maybe you still feel a sort of . . . loyalty to your old teacher that would prevent you from bringing him to trial if it turned out he had gone down the wrong road."

"What does that mean?" Longarm asked, his eyes turning suspicious.

"Do you know anything about what he's been doing since he was fired from this agency?"

"I heard he went back to a bounty hunter."

"That's correct." Billy turned back to face Longarm. "From what I've heard, he's operated the same way as a

4

private bounty hunter as he acted for us . . . only on his own, he somehow came across a great deal of money."

Longarm's eyebrows raised in surprise. "How'd he do that?"

"I don't know, but my source in Arizona said that he mysteriously came into possession of a very prosperous gold mine and that the former owner has never been found or heard from again."

"Come on!" Longarm protested. "You're not suggesting that Jesse murdered a mine owner and somehow managed to gain title to the claim."

"Well, you know as well as I do that Jesse Jerome spent his money as fast as it came into his hands."

"Okay, he likes to gamble," Longarm admitted. "Jesse probably won his gold mine playing cards. That happens plenty of times. A fella starts out with just a few dollars in his pockets, goes on a winning streak, and by dawn he's a wealthy, wealthy man."

"Sure," Billy agreed. "That can happen. Only thing is . . . Jesse Jerome was a terrible gambler. You know that as well as I do. He always thought he was good, but he wasn't."

Longarm scowled. "Well, that is true, but sometimes Lady Luck comes a-callin' and it doesn't matter how bad you are because when she smiles, you come up winners."

"Custis, do you remember that time that Jesse had a can of deadly scorpions and he tossed them onto a card table down at the Palace Club right here in Denver? He was drunk, had lost all his money, and he wanted to scare the bejeezus out of the people who'd won his money."

"I remember. I wasn't there, but I read about it in the newspaper. I guess he did what he set out to do." Longarm had to smile. "Diamond Jim Brady was stung pretty bad by those scorpions and damned near died."

"That was the last straw, and why this department finally said enough is enough and fired him."

"So Jesse Jerome is a little crazy when he is drinking

and gets mad," Longarm said. "The man saved my life *twice*. I'm willing to give him the benefit of the doubt."

"I was afraid you'd say that." Billy managed a tight smile and climbed to his feet. "Custis, I'm sorry that I pulled you in here for this assignment. Go on back and have a great time down in Santa Fe with that *señorita*. I'll send Homer Wilson to Arizona to investigate the Scorpion Murders."

"Scorpion Murders," Longarm echoed. "What the deuce are you talking about?"

"Apparently, you don't read the newspapers."

"Not lately," Longarm admitted.

"Well, if you did, you'd know that no less than the territorial governor of Arizona was found dead in his bed a few days ago, and do you know what they found crawling all over his body?"

"Scorpions?"

"That's right. Someone had put them into his bed while he was staying at the Agate Hotel in Agate, Arizona. Apparently, the governor was drunk and by the time the scorpions got done stinging him, he was bloated and turning purple with their poison."

Longarm was accustomed to all sorts of deaths, but hearing about this one made his skin crawl. "Hell of a way to go," he muttered.

"It was. And get this . . . it turns out that a reporter from Tucson who was up there doing the story wrote an article strongly hinting that Jesse Jerome had put the scorpions in the governor's bed. And do you know what happened to that brave but foolish reporter?"

"No," Longarm said, thinking he could guess.

"The reporter was found the next day tied spread-eagled to the four-poster bed of his hotel room with scorpions crawling all over his dead body!"

"Holy shit," Longarm drawled, shaking his head. "Now I see why they are calling it the Scorpion Murders."

"Yeah, and now you know why we think that your old

friend and teacher Jesse Jerome—now wealthy mine owner and respectable Agate, Arizona, businessman—is behind those murders."

"I don't share that opinion."

Billy Vail sat down heavily. He leaned his short, chubby arms on his desk and said, "And that's why I'm sending Deputy Marshal Homer Wilson to Agate, Arizona, instead of you."

"Now wait just a darned minute here! Are you saying I don't have enough integrity as a sworn officer of the law to arrest Jesse Jerome if I learn he is guilty?"

"Yeah," Billy said quietly. "I guess that I am."

Longarm was not a man to lose his temper unless the situation was extreme. And this situation was extreme. "Dammit, Billy, have I ever let my personal feelings interfere with my job? Even once in all the years I've been deputized do you *ever* remember that happening!"

"No," Billy said calmly, "I don't. But after listening to what you've just told me, I'm afraid that this would be the exception. That you wouldn't bring Jesse Jerome to justice . . . even if you were convinced he was guilty of the Scorpion Murders."

"That just about ties it!" Longarm shouted. "I thought you knew me better."

"Let's not put your integrity to the test," Billy replied. "I'll send Homer Wilson to Agate tomorrow. Go on down to Santa Fe and have your well-deserved vacation."

Ignoring Longarm's glare, Billy looked down at a stack of paperwork and said, "I've got a couple of reports to do now. Thanks for coming in. I really appreciate it."

Longarm jumped up in anger and stomped to the door. He started to leave, then changed his mind and marched back to Billy's desk. He leaned on it hard and said, "Look me in the eye, Billy. Look me in the eye and tell me that you're wrong."

Billy raised his head. "Maybe I am, but I'm not willing to take a chance on it. Jesse Jerome saved your life twice

7

and you feel bound to honor that, no matter what he might have done or become after leaving Colorado and the service of this agency. So I'll send Wilson."

"Wilson is inept! He's an idiot!"

"He tries hard and he's a bit slow, but he will do his duty."

"And so would I!"

"I . . . I have my doubts."

"Well, if that doesn't just tie it!" Longarm raged. "By gawd, I'll go to Agate, Arizona, and I'll see Jesse Jerome and get to the bottom of those Scorpion Murders. And I'll arrest Jesse—if he's guilty—and see that he goes to trial."

"Jesse wouldn't like that. He'd call in the debt you owe to him. Make no mistake about that, Custis. And when he did, how do you know that you wouldn't fold and let him off? Maybe convince yourself that he was somehow innocent even though all the facts pointed to him being the Scorpion Murderer?"

Longarm sat down. "Look. It's because I know the man that I have to go to Arizona and clear his name. Sure, he tossed scorpions on the faro table at the Palace Club. But he was drunk and I'm damn sure that he'd been cheated out of a pile of money."

"That was never proven."

"Maybe not," Longarm admitted. "But Diamond Jim Brady died in a shoot-out and they found aces up his bloody sleeve. He was a slick card shark and more than a match for Jesse and anyone else playing a straight and honest game."

"So you'll go?"

"Jesse would eat Homer Wilson for breakfast. Wilson wouldn't have a chance if it turned out wrong."

"But you would?"

Longarm took a deep breath. "Jesse is a bit past his prime. I could take him if I had to make the arrest."

"And if he resisted?"

"Then," Longarm promised, "I'd do what I had to do."

"All right then," Billy Vail said, reaching into his desk and dragging out stage and railroad tickets and a thick wad of greenbacks for Longarm's travel expenses. "You're booked on the stage due to roll first thing tomorrow morning. Good luck and be damned careful."

Custis Long stared at the money and tickets, then at his boss. "Did you have this all planned out? The argument and what I'd say and everything?"

"No," Billy said. "I had hoped you'd just agree to go to Agate, Arizona, and investigate the allegations against Jesse Jerome. It's not a federal case, but the acting territorial governor just happens to be an old friend of the head of our agency. Naturally, he is scared half to death about sharing the same fate as his predecessor and that reporter."

"That seems damned unlikely."

"Maybe. Maybe not. But put yourself in his place. How would you like the possibility of waking up some dark night with deadly scorpions crawling all over your body?"

Despite himself, Longarm shivered.

Chapter 2

Longarm went back to his room and slept until evening, then dressed and headed out to find a good steak for dinner. He was well known in his neighborhood, and nodded to many acquaintances as he walked down the sidewalk toward the Copper Cafe, where the food was good and the prices were reasonable. The cafe was not in the best neighborhood, but Longarm figured it was good to stop in frequently just so everyone understood that he had an interest in keeping the area safe.

Stepping into the cafe, he waved a greeting to the owner, who also doubled as the cook, and to Milly, his waitress. Milly was a pretty red-haired Irish girl, and her boss was a burly, middle-aged Englishman named Rory who knew how to cook a steak just right and do wonders with potatoes and vegetables.

"Evening, Marshal," Milly said as he sat down in the crowded diner at a little table near the back of the room. "How are you today?"

"I'm just fine," he replied, removing his snuff-brown Stetson with its flat rim and crown. He draped his coat over the back of his chair, and couldn't help but notice that Milly was looking exceptionally fetching this evening. "But I'm heading off for Arizona in the morning."

"Arizona?" Milly shook her head. "I thought you were going down to Santa Fe for a little fun and relaxation."

"That was my intention until the government convinced me otherwise. How are the steaks tonight?"

"We got some prime ones tonight. Beef stew is also pretty special and half the price."

"I'll have a beer to start with, then my usual steak, potatoes, corn, coffee, and apple pie for dessert."

"I'll pick out the biggest and juiciest of the steaks for you, Marshal. You still look to be on the lean side. You need to fatten up like my boss!"

She said that last part loud enough that Rory overhead. Sticking his head out of the kitchen, the Englishman shouted, "Don't you be listening to her now! She's full of it as usual!"

Longarm drank two beers while he waited, and when Milly brought his dinner, the steak was so big, thick, and juicy that he actually sighed with contentment.

"Hope it is to your liking," the pretty Irish gal said as she went to serve a couple of new customers. Longarm heard her ask, "What can we get for you boys this evening? Steaks are our specialty, but the Irish stew is mighty tasty and filling."

"I want a big bowl of chili," the larger of the pair demanded, his words angry and slurred from drinking. "I don't want no damned steak or stew. Chili."

"Take it easy, John," the smaller man said. "She ain't to blame."

"We don't have chili on the menu tonight," Milly explained. "How about some hash or—"

"Gawdammit, woman, are you deaf?" John shouted.

Longarm laid his knife and fork down, and was just about to come to his feet when Rory burst out of the kitchen. "Get out of here!" he bellowed. "I don't need your business!"

The big man started to come out of his chair bellowing,

"Mister, you and this dumb bitch can go straight to hell!"

Rory punched the man named John in the side of the head, knocking him out of his chair. Then he turned to the other man at the table and shouted, "I said to get out . . . both of you!"

"All right," the other one agreed. "Just take it easy there. We're going."

"You'd better do it quick or I'll give you what I just gave to your friend."

Rory turned to Milly. "Never mind them. They're just liquored up and ignorant."

"I know that," she said.

Suddenly, John raised a pistol, took aim, and fired. Longarm had just started to pick up his knife and fork when the shot boomed out, and he saw Rory spin around, grabbing his shoulder. The shooter thumbed back the hammer of his six-gun, and would have shot Rory dead, but Milly hurled a glass of beer at John, sending his second shot into the ceiling. By then Longarm was on his feet, knocking over his table and drawing his gun. Customers dived for cover, some throwing themselves out the door as Longarm tried to get his sights on the drunk who'd just shot Rory.

He would have killed John except that Milly attacked like a wildcat, ripping and tearing at the drunken man's face. The big man cursed and knocked Milly aside, then took aim at Rory.

Longarm didn't have time to aim . . . and it wasn't necessary anyhow. He fired from waist level, aiming a bit low so that his slug tore into John's diaphragm, just below the rib cage. The man screamed and tried to fire back at Longarm, but a second bullet struck him under the chin and exited through the back of his skull.

"You killed him!" the other man cried. "You killed my brother!"

Longarm brought the barrel of his Colt .44-.40 to bear on the smaller man's chest. "Don't do anything stupid."

"But you killed him!" the man wailed.

"Put your hands over your head!" Longarm ordered.

Instead, the distraught man reached for his gun. Longarm could have drilled him twice before he'd even cleared leather, but instead he took two steps forward and pistol-whipped the man across the forehead.

It was over.

Milly rushed to her boss, who was still on his feet, but dazed and in obvious shock.

"Let's have a look at that shoulder wound," Longarm said, easing the cafe owner into a chair. He helped Rory remove his ruined shirt. "Milly, get something to plug up the hole and we'll help him down to Dr. Blake's office. He'll have him patched up in no time."

Milly returned a moment later with clean dish towels, which they used to bandage the wound and then make a sling for the arm and shoulder.

"Is it broken?" Rory asked, his face pale and his hands shaky.

"I don't think so," Longarm replied.

"I don't know what we'd have done without you," Milly told Longarm. "We'd *both* be dead. And I ask you, for what? For lack of a bowl of damned chili!"

Longarm took a deep breath. "I don't understand it either. But I'm sure that the chili had nothing to do with that man drawing his gun and firing at your boss. Something else was eating at him and maybe—when his brother wakes up in jail—he can tell us."

"Milly," Rory said, "why don't you invite our customers back to finish their meals? The marshal can get me down to the doctor and then come back and haul these two off."

Longarm surveyed the room and said in a loud voice to the customers just now climbing off the floor, "You all saw what happened. Instead of a refund, it would be neighborly to pass a hat around and take up a collection for Rory. What do you boys say?"

To a man, the twenty or so customers agreed, and a hat was quickly passed around the cafe. Men righted their overturned tables and chairs. Some made a big show of going back to eating as if nothing unusual had happened at the Copper Cafe.

"See?" Longarm said in a low voice as he helped Rory out the door. "There's a lot more good ones around than bad. I wouldn't be surprised if you doubled your normal take on tips tonight, Milly."

Tears were running down her cheeks. "I sure am thankful you were here tonight. Don't suppose we could hire you as assistant cook, huh?"

Despite the grim circumstances, Longarm smiled when he shook his head no.

An hour later, he had the big man in the undertaker's office being fitted for a wooden box and the smaller brother locked up in a nearby jail. The Denver policeman on duty shook his head when Longarm told him the circumstances.

"Marshal Long, I just don't know what people are coming to these days. Seems like they just go crazy for no reason."

"Pour a bucket of water over your prisoner," Longarm said. "I want to ask him what set his brother off that way."

The policeman, whose name was Carl, got a bucket of water and stepped into the cell. He poured a full bucket over the unconscious man and when he sputtered into wakefulness, dragged the prisoner up on the hard cell cot and held him upright while Longarm grabbed his hair and bounced his head against the wall.

"Hey," Longarm ordered. "Wake up and talk!"

The man's eyes popped open, but they didn't seem to be focused, so Longarm turned to Carl and said, "Douse him a second time."

"But his mouth is open and he might drown," Carl protested.

15

"Too bad. Do what I say."

Carl went outside and dipped the bucket into a horse-watering trough. He came back in and pitched all of it into the man's face.

Now the man was wide awake. There was a huge goose egg rising on his forehead where the heavy barrel of Longarm's Colt had hit him earlier.

"What's your full name?" Longarm asked.

"George Pickett."

"What was your big brother's name?"

"John Pickett."

"Why'd he go crazy and shoot that cook?"

"You heard it. He wanted chili."

"That's not good enough."

George took a deep, shuddering breath and said, "My brother lost a year's wages playing cards up the street. He was cheated and when we tried to get our money back, we was beat up."

"So your brother comes into the Copper Cafe and tries to get even?"

"John had a bad, bad temper."

"Well," Longarm said, stepping back and shaking his head, "his bad temper got him killed. And you're going to spend a long time in jail for not throwing up your hands when I gave the order."

"Don't matter to me anymore," George said, wiping water from his face and then cradling his head between his hands. "When Pa finds out what happened, he'd kill me anyways for not saving my brother."

"Where are you from?" Carl asked, shaking a big ring of jail keys.

"Texas. Me and my brother used to be cowboys, but we turned to mining up in Cripple Creek."

"You should have stayed in Texas and kept cowboying," Longarm said bluntly.

"Yes, sir. We sure should have. Now, Pa will want John's body shipped back to El Paso, but I ain't got no

16

money to do it." George wiped water from his dripping face. "How am I ever going to get my brother's body back to Texas?"

"You aren't," Longarm told the former cowboy. "All I know is that you'll see a judge tomorrow and he'll make sure that you have plenty of time to think about what happens when a man takes out his anger on someone who is innocent."

"Thanks for not killing me too, Marshal. I reckon you could have if you'd wanted."

"That's right." Longarm stepped out of the cell. "Carl, I'd better write down what I saw while you go on back to the Copper Cafe and get signed statements from witnesses."

"Will you be able to testify at a hearing tomorrow?" the policeman asked. "Judge Walter takes a shooting death pretty serious."

"So do I," Longarm snapped. "But tell the judge that I had urgent business in Agate, Arizona. If he needs more than what I'm writing down, then he'll have to wait until I get back."

"How long might that be . . . in case the judge asks?"

"Damned if I know," Longarm replied. "I need to find out who's killing people with scorpions."

Carl's jaw sagged. "What!"

"Never mind," Longarm told the shocked Denver policeman. "It's a long story and one I'm not entirely sure I believe myself."

And so, without another word of comment or explanation, Longarm sat down at a desk and began to write.

Chapter 3

It was nearly ten o'clock when Longarm finished writing up a report for the judge. He hadn't finished his supper and he was hungry and a mite dejected because killing a man was always a terrible waste. He would have thought that, given all the men he'd been forced to kill, he would get used to it . . . but he hadn't. If he ever got to the point where it didn't bother him, it would be time to find another line of work.

"Carl?"

"Yeah?" the policeman said, raising his head up from his cot.

"Did you get the dead man to the mortuary?"

"Sure did."

"What about the witnesses?"

"I got statements from those that were still at the Copper Cafe. Most had left, but there were three or four whose names and accounts I wrote down for the judge."

"Good."

Carl sat up on his bunk. He was about Longarm's age, but short and kind of pudgy. "Marshal Long, them fellas at the cafe said they never seen a man shuck his six-gun as fast as you did when you shot John Pickett. They say your hand moved so fast that no one actually even saw you draw that Colt."

"That's because they were all diving for cover."

"How many men have you killed?"

Longarm got up and stretched. "I don't keep count. How many have you killed?"

"One," Carl admitted. "He was coming at me with a knife and I had no choice. But if he'd have had a gun, he'd have probably killed me."

"Why?"

"Because I'm not that good with a side arm. I'm a fair rifle shot, but can't hit anything with my pistol."

Longarm frowned. "Carl, my advice is to practice your aim and draw. One of these days—and you can count on this—you'll either live or die depending on your skill with a gun."

"I suppose you're right."

"I know I'm right," Longarm told the man. "I wouldn't have hired you, much less kept you on the payroll, knowing you were a poor shot with a six-gun. Start practicing before it's too late."

"I got a chance to manage a feed store," the man said. "They'd pay me the same as the wages I get here. I dunno. Maybe I should take that job."

Longarm agreed completely. He'd seen so many who loved the authority but lacked the skill or the nerve to back it up when the chips were down. Carl struck him as exactly that kind.

"What do you think, Marshal Long?"

"I think you're in the wrong line of work and should take the feed store job before someone ventilates your gizzard."

Carl took a deep breath and nodded. "I believe I'll do that one of these days. Yes, sir. I believe that I will!"

"Don't put it off," Longarm warned. "A lawman never knows when he'll walk into a room or someplace and have to defend his life."

"Just like you did tonight."

"That's right," Longarm answered. "I'm leaving. I'll stop by the Copper Cafe and make sure that Milly is all right."

"She's fine," Carl said, coming to his feet. "I talked to her a little while ago and she's pretty nervous, but I guess that's to be expected. Hell, look at my own hands. See how they're shaking? And I wasn't even there when the bullets started flying!"

Carl held out his hands and they really were shaking. Longarm shook his head. "Turn in your badge first thing tomorrow. Like I said a few minutes ago, you're in the wrong business."

"I swear I will."

Longarm left the jail and went down to the Copper Cafe. The street was pretty much deserted because there weren't any saloons or bars close by. When he reached the cafe, he saw a "Closed" sign in the window. He peered inside and saw Milly cleaning up, and he knocked on the front door, causing her to jump and spill a tray of cups and plates. Whirling around, she looked frightened until she recognized Longarm.

"You scared me half to death," she told him as she unlocked the front door and let him inside. "Look at the mess I made, Marshal."

"I'll help you clean up," he said. "Where's a broom and dustpan?"

"I'll do it," Milly said. "You never got to finish your steak. Why don't I fry you up a new one right now."

"Too much trouble."

"Not for the man that saved Rory's life and probably my own as well."

"Suit yourself," Longarm said. "I still am hungry."

"I couldn't eat a thing," Milly confessed. "My stomach is tied up in knots. I'm going to have a glass of whiskey to settle my nerves. Want one while you wait for dinner?"

"Sure, but not a whole glassful."

Longarm insisted on cleaning up the broken dishes and glassware while Milly make him another steak dinner. After that, they sat together at the table with the "Closed" sign still on the door.

"You cook 'em even better than Rory," he said with a smile.

"Thank you!" Milly took another swallow of her whiskey. "I sure do owe you plenty. So does Rory."

"Forget it," Longarm said. "It's my job."

"Not here it wasn't. You were off duty, weren't you?"

"I'm never off duty," he replied. "Over the years, I've arrested and shot too many men to ever drop my guard."

Milly leaned her elbows on the table and studied his face. "Do you like killing people?"

"Of course not!"

"I'm sorry. That was a dumb question. I guess the whiskey is already affecting my brain."

"You went through a lot this evening." Longarm finished his steak and added, "But the important thing is that you showed courage when you had to and acted without hesitation. If you hadn't attacked John Pickett, he'd have killed Rory for sure before I could get a bead on him."

"You think so?"

"I'm sure of it. You're the one that saved Rory, not me."

"Oh, we both did."

Longarm dug into his apple pie. "Did you happen to bake this?"

"I sure did. Rory is good with meat and vegetables, but I'm an expert with cakes and pies."

Longarm smacked his lips, and when he'd polished off the last crumbs and then washed it all down with whiskey, he said, "You're a handsome lass and a brave one to boot."

"And you, Marshal, are also handsome and brave. No wonder you have such a reputation as a ladies' man."

Longarm leaned back in his chair and found a cigar in his vest pocket. "Mind if I smoke?"

"You could do anything you want, Marshal."

He had started to light his cigar, but the look in her eye caused him to pause and then grin. "Anything?" he asked.

"Yes." She giggled and had a little more whiskey. "Shall we lock up and go into the kitchen?"

"What for?"

"Rory has a bed in the back room. He takes a nap sometimes when business is slow in the afternoons."

"You don't say!"

"I do say." Milly reached across the table and took his hand. "Come with me, you big, brave, and handsome hunk of man."

Longarm followed Milly through the kitchen like a puppy at the end of a leash. They found the bed, and when Milly lit a candle and slowly undressed, he felt his manhood start to push urgently at the inside of his trousers.

"Milly," he said, cupping her large, firm breasts in his palms. "You're one hell of a beautiful Irish girl."

"I'm an Irish woman," she corrected. "But just in case you aren't fully convinced, let me show you."

She removed his gunbelt, then his vest, tie, and shirt. Her hands were soft and quick and cool as she unbuttoned Longarm's trousers and eased him down on the bed a moment before she removed his boots, socks, and every last stitch of his clothing.

"My, oh, my," she breathed, staring at his manhood standing so tall and so proud. "You got a real big one!"

"Can you handle it?" he asked.

"Just watch me," Milly said, throwing a leg over him and then hanging poised just above. She put her finger to her own honey pot and breathed in deeply. "I'm wet and ready, Marshal."

"Under the circumstances," he said, "why don't you just call me Custis."

"All right, Custis. How does *this* feel?"

Longarm sighed with pleasure as Milly sort of slid down on his manhood and enfolded it into her hot wetness. He lay still as she began to slowly move up and down on him, head back, long red hair hanging over her breasts, until he pushed it back and began to use his lips and tongue on her hard nipples.

"What do you think now, Marshal? Girl ... or woman?"

"Woman. Definitely woman," he panted, filling his mouth with her breast and sucking until she squirmed and began to hump faster and harder.

Longarm's powerful hands grabbed her slender hips, and he began to thrust and jam his manhood deeper into her body. Milly moaned and thrashed and threw her long hair around, until Longarm rolled her onto her back and really began to thrust.

"Oh, Marshal, have mercy!" she cried. "Have mercy!"

Longarm growled deep in his throat and pumped even harder, until Milly was screaming so loud that she could have been heard out in the empty Denver street. Then suddenly, her eyes opened wide, her legs shivered like leaves in the wind, and her body started convulsing in the throes of great passion.

Longarm waited until she was locked up tight on his manhood and quivering. Then his lips pulled back from his teeth and he began filling her with his hot, spurting seed.

They went at it twice more before they crawled out of the bed and Milly fixed him breakfast early the next morning.

"How long are you going to be in Arizona?" Milly asked, rubbing up against him like a contented kitten.

"I'm afraid that I can't rightly say."

"Will you come here looking for me?"

He hugged her tight. "Now that just depends, Milly."

"Depends on what?"

"If you let me close up this cafe with you again or not."

"You bet I will!"

"Then I'll be back as fast as I can," Longarm promised over his first cup of coffee. "Count on it."

"I will," Milly replied. "And don't you get too tired in Arizona to satisfy this Irish woman."

"Not a chance," he said, thinking he had better get back to his own rooms and do some fast packing before he had to leave for Agate, Arizona.

Chapter 4

It took Longarm eight days to reach Arizona using a combination of stagecoaches and railroads. When he reached Prescott, the territorial capital, he got a room at the St. Michael's Hotel on Whiskey Row and rested for a day before inquiring as to the whereabouts of Agate.

"It's about twenty miles northeast of us," the hotel desk clerk said. "But I don't think you're going to want to go there and stay."

"Why is that?"

"Well, haven't you heard about the Scorpion Murders?"

It was Longarm's practice to often feign ignorance in order to get people talking and maybe hear something important he didn't know about. "Hmmm," he mused, "seems like I did hear something about deadly scorpions."

"Well, I should hope so," the clerk said, looking down his bifocals at the registration ledger. "And I feel it's my duty to tell you that Agate is not a good town to visit."

"Because of the Scorpion Murders?"

"Of course. Why would anyone want to risk their lives in that town?"

"I have business there so I have no choice," Longarm

27

told the man. "Can you recommend any particular Agate hotel?"

"I wouldn't sleep a wink in any of them. Most people here in Prescott feel the same way as I do. Agate is an embarrassment for the territory. You know, we'd like to be granted statehood someday, but that's not going to happen if we keep getting bad publicity. Can you tell me why anyone would use scorpions to kill their enemies?"

"Low risk," Longarm suggested. "All you'd have to do is have a passkey to sneak into a man's room at night, and then you just dump a few of the little jaspers into the bed and . . . bam! No more enemy."

The desk clerk shivered. "Hell of a way to go, that's for sure. I'd rather be shot than stung to death by a bed full of vipers."

Longarm saw nothing to be gained by trying to explain that scorpions were more like big spiders and bugs than they were like snakes.

"Where is the best place to eat in Prescott?"

"We serve three excellent meals a day at a reasonable price. Dinner is at seven."

"Thanks. Is there a stage that goes to Agate?"

"Yes, and it leaves every morning at nine A.M. sharp. I can assure you that you won't have much company. Quite a few people are leaving that town for good."

"Does anyone have any idea who is behind the murders?"

"Most of us think that it has to be big Jesse Jerome. He is neither trusted nor well liked in these parts."

"Why is that?"

"He ran for mayor of Prescott and lost. So then he ran for town marshal and we voted him down for that too."

"Couldn't handle it, huh?"

The hotel desk clerk shook his head. "Actually, Jesse Jerome would have made one hell of a good town marshal. But nobody here in Prescott trusts or likes the man. He's got a foul temper, drinks and gambles too much.

I've seen him in our hotel saloon a time or two, and he's not welcome back."

"Is Jerome down and out?"

"Hardly! He owns half of Agate and one of the wealthiest gold mines in the territory." The desk clerk leaned forward. "But everyone feels that he killed the former owner to gain title."

"Then why wasn't he arrested?"

"No one wanted to get killed. Our own marshal was ordered by the city council to arrest Jerome and bring him in for a hearing before the judge. And do you know what?"

"What?" Longarm asked.

"He resigned rather than face Jerome. Not that anyone blamed him, because he'd have gotten plugged. Jerome isn't a man who would stand for being arrested. No, sir! With that man, you'd better be ready to shoot it out, or he'll send you packing with your tail between your legs."

"He sounds like a real ripsnorter," Longarm said. "Any real evidence to show he killed the former mine owner or poured scorpions in the bed of the governor and that newspaper reporter?"

"So, you do know a thing or two about the Scorpion Murders."

"Just what I've heard in the saloon and on the street," Longarm answered. "But you know that kind of talk isn't very reliable."

"Well, I would say that it was reliable if people told you Jesse Jerome is as guilty as sin. Make no bones about it. The evidence might be lacking to tie him to the killings, but he's guilty, all right!"

Longarm clucked his tongue as if in agreement, but said, "Thing of it is, our United States Constitution guarantees us the right to be considered innocent until we are proven guilty."

The desk clerk scoffed. "Jesse Jerome is riding high, but he's as crooked as a sidewinder and ten times as dan-

29

gerous. You mark my words and remember them well. There will be more Scorpion Murders. Yes, sir. You can bet your poke on it, and that's why I'd strongly advise you to stay clear of Agate."

"Thanks for your advice."

"You're welcome," the desk clerk said, "but I have the feeling you're not going to use it."

"I have no choice but to go to Agate."

"Then I wish you good luck. And when you go to bed at night, be sure and lock your door."

"I will," Longarm assured the man.

Custis went outside and walked around the famous Whiskey Row, across from which was a plaza, government office, and courthouse. There were huge shade trees and lots of grass. He hadn't been to Prescott before, but he liked the looks of the town and would much have preferred to stay there rather than go on to Agate. He was anxious to see his old friend and mentor, but also apprehensive to think that all the rumors and accusations about Jesse being behind the killings might be true.

"I'll just assume he is innocent until I learn otherwise," Longarm told himself as he went off in search of a good saloon where he might hear even more about Jesse and the scorpions.

Longarm had an uneventful evening and slept very well that night. Nine o'clock in the morning found him on his way across the Prescott Valley toward the eastern mountains with only three other passengers on board the stage. One was a minister, an austere-looking man in his midforties who tried to convert Longarm to his fellowship in Agate. The second was a drummer who sold boots and belts of low quality, and the third was a charming woman in her early thirties named Carol Dunn, who was married to a cattle rancher and who lived about six miles north of Agate.

"And what is your line of business?" Carol asked after

they had talked about weather, cattle, and the general state of affairs.

Longarm had no wish to lie, but neither did he think it was in his best interests to reveal the true purpose of his visit to Agate, Arizona. So he said, "I'm just looking for fresh opportunities."

Carol had a heart-shaped face and pretty brown eyes. She would have been very interesting if Longarm hadn't learned that she was not only married but had two small children. She smiled and asked, "What kind of opportunities?"

"Oh," Longarm said, shrugging his broad shoulders. "I like to look at . . . land. Yes."

"Are you interested in ranch land?"

"Yes, as well as mining properties."

"Well," Carol said smiling as if she had finally figured him out, "there are a lot of good mining prospects in these mountains. You've no doubt heard that a man named Jesse Jerome has made a fortune in gold mining."

"I heard about that."

"Now, I'm not going to say that he *deserves* to have made that fortune. But that's the reality of it."

"I understand that Mr. Jerome owns quite a few other businesses in Agate."

The minister, whose name Longarm had already forgotten, snipped, "Mr. Jerome is the reincarnation of Satan! Before that man came to Agate, we had a nice town. Now, we're the Sodom of the West! Something has to be done to stop him before he ruins everyone!"

"I see," Longarm replied, watching Mrs. Dunn to see if she agreed. But she had no comment or reaction. "I've heard about the Scorpion Murders."

The drummer paled a little. "You can be sure that I'm not sleeping in the Agate Hotel this or any other night!"

"Well," Longarm said, "I will be. I'll just lock my door, and I sleep light. Besides, I'm not important enough to be murdered."

31

"You hope," the salesman said. "Who can say which of us might be the next victim? Perhaps the killer is crazy!"

"Gentlemen, could we please talk about something else?" Carol asked. "I see no need for wild speculations and for unduly alarming each other."

"That's easy for you to say," the minister snipped. "You and your family live out at your ranch and so are safe. It's those of us in Agate that have to worry who might be the next one murdered. I pray that this is all over, but who knows!"

Not much was said the rest of the way into Agate, which was up in the mountains. It was an attractive enough community possessing an air of former prosperity. There were the usual saloons, cafes, and livery stables that were the backbone businesses of all small Western towns. Agate was carved out of forest, and Longarm saw evidence of a sawmill as well as mining activity.

"This looks like a nice place," he commented to no one in particular.

"It used to be," the minister snapped. "Until the arrival of Jesse Jerome."

"You'd better be careful of what you say," Mrs. Dunn warned quietly.

"I speak out against that man every chance I have," the minister replied, voice shaking with anger. "Evil is evil and it doesn't matter that it comes in fancy trappings. Jesse Jerome is a godless man. He never even attends church."

"Neither do I," Carol Dunn said tartly. "But I don't consider myself or my husband evil . . . or godless."

"Hmph!" the minister snorted. "That's more the pity!"

Longarm saw the woman's cheeks flush with anger. The salesman looked away, and then they were rolling down Agate's main street. Upon closer inspection, Longarm noticed that quite a few of the shops and businesses were boarded up.

32

"Things look to be on the decline here," he said.

The minister fumed in silence, but Carol Dunn was ready with a reply. "Jesse Jerome has scared off a lot of people. When they leave, he buys their shops and buildings. I think he is just waiting to buy up nearly everything in town before he changes his colors and tries to lure merchants back to Agate. But of course, then they'll have to pay him rent or buy town sites from the scoundrel."

"I see," Longarm mused aloud. "Diabolical."

"That's Mr. Jerome in a word," the woman agreed as their stagecoach came to a stop before the Agate Hotel.

They all disembarked, and Mrs. Dunn hurried over to a buckboard driven by a man, who gave her a kiss on the cheek and then helped her up to a seat. A few minutes later, the woman and her husband drove out of town. The drummer headed for the nearest saloon, and the minister shouted at Longarm, "Pray for us, stranger! Pray for the deliverance of this town from the forces of Satan!"

Longarm nodded, gathered his bags, and made his way to the Agate Hotel. The lobby was quite tasteful, with nice rugs arranged across a well-polished hardwood floor. There were head mounts of a moose, an clk, and a bear on the walls, and the furniture was of the finest quality. All in all, it was one of the most pleasant hotel lobbies that Longarm had seen in years, and he judged that the individual rooms ought to be quite nice.

He had to ring a bell at the registration desk several times before a woman appeared who was so striking that Longarm openly stared. She was dark-complected, and his first impression was that she was mulatto or at least part Indian. She was tall and statuesque, with long black hair that was braided and hung in a thick rope to her slender waist. Her eyes were the color of acorns and her lips were full and sensuous. Her movement was graceful, her step light, and her brown skin was perfect.

"Hello there," she said without a smile or any warmth

as she paused behind the hotel registration desk. "Can I help you?"

"I'd like a room."

"A room?"

"Yes, this is a hotel, isn't it?"

"Of course. It's just that we haven't had many guests lately. Our rates are two dollars a night and you can go upstairs and take any room on the second floor."

Two dollars was double the rate he'd expected, but then, this was a far nicer hotel than expected, so the price seemed fair. Longarm picked up the pen beside the register and wrote his name and that he was from Denver. "There," he told her as he laid a twenty-dollar gold piece on the counter. "That will get us started."

"You're staying for *ten* days?"

"Yes. Maybe less, but perhaps even a bit longer."

"I see." She turned the register around. "And you are Mr. Custis Long."

He could tell that she was aching to know the nature of his visit, but Longarm purposely kept that to himself. She and the rest of the town would learn soon enough that he was a United States deputy marshal, and they'd quickly guess his reason for coming to Agate.

"Well, Mr. Long. I do hope you enjoy your visit to Agate."

"I'm not here for pleasure."

"Oh, business then?"

"That's right."

"That's . . . that's very interesting," she said, trying to read his face. "And by the way, if you just happen to be looking to purchase a hotel, then let me be the first to inform you that mine is for sale . . . at a *very* reasonable price."

"I'm sorry, but I'm not interested in hotels, even one as obviously well kept as yours."

"Too bad," she told him, with a shrug of her shoulders. "But then, you'll soon discover that most of this town that

34

hasn't been gobbled up by Mr. Jerome is for sale at extremely attractive prices."

"Where can I find him?"

"Mr. Jerome?"

"That's right."

"His office is just up the street. It's the one with a sign that says, 'Sheriff's Office,' and has a jail. He's expanded the building next door. But Jerome still likes to do business in the sheriff's part of it for reasons that he alone understands."

"Thank you," Longarm said, tipping his hat. "And you are?"

"Mrs. Delia Ballou."

"Good day to you and Mr. Ballou, and I'm sure that I will enjoy my stay here."

"I certainly hope so."

Longarm studied her for a moment, aware that, in addition to her great beauty, there was a deep sadness in the woman. It caused him to wonder, but he said nothing more as he turned on his heel and climbed the stairway up to the second floor. He did not look back down into the lobby at Mrs. Ballou, but he would have bet anything she was staring at him, her beautiful face reflecting curiosity.

Chapter 5

There were six rooms upstairs, all of them nicely decorated. Longarm took 203, the one farthest down the hallway, with a window overlooking Agate's main street. He unpacked his bags and took a nap. When he awoke later that afternoon, he shaved and changed his shirt, then headed downstairs.

"Is everything all right?" Mrs. Ballou asked from behind the desk.

"It's just mighty lonesome up there."

"I'm afraid that I can't help you with that. Would you like to take a bath later?"

"As a matter of fact, I would."

"Just let me know when so long as it isn't at supper time, and I'll fill a tub in the room at the end of the hallway."

"I'd appreciate that."

The woman smiled and disappeared into what Longarm figured was her and her husband's living quarters. He went outside and stood on the boardwalk, surveying the town for a few minutes and thinking about what he'd say to his old friend and mentor, Jesse Jerome. Could Jesse really have gone bad and be responsible for the Scorpion

Murders? Longarm sure hoped not. It would be hard to arrest a man who had saved your life not once ... but twice. Still, he was sworn to uphold the law, and that he would do if necessary.

"Sure hope Jesse ain't gone bad," Longarm muttered to himself as he produced a cigar and jammed it into his mouth. He chewed the end of the cigar and started down the street, forgetting to light the stogie because he was so preoccupied with memories of Jesse Jerome.

When he reached the sheriff's office, he let himself in and saw two men seated at desks. They were both tough-looking characters, and they eyed him suspiciously for several moments.

"I'm looking for Jesse," Longarm said when they offered no greeting or introductions.

"And who might you be?" the one with the double chins and gravy stains on his shirt demanded to know.

"I'm an old friend."

"Name?"

"Jesse would remember me as Longarm."

The other man barked a laugh. "Longarm? What the hell kind of a stupid name is that?"

"It's the name of a lawman, you idiot. Now where is Jesse?"

The one he'd called an idiot started to jump up, but Longarm flashed his badge and said, "I'm a federal marshal and you'd better stay right where you're at and mind your manners."

"Luke, you'd better do as the big, bad federal marshal says," the other one suggested.

Luke eased back down in his chair. "I don't take kindly to a personal insult, and the fact that you might be a federal lawman don't mean a damn thing to me."

"That's because you're big on talk and short on brains," Longarm replied. "Now, I'm only going to ask you boys nice once more ... where is Jesse?"

"He's up at the mine," the other man, who had the look

of a dandy, with long curly brown hair and clothes that stamped him as either a professional gambler or gunman, said. "He'll be up there for the next day or two. I'm Deputy Frank Curry and my friend here is Deputy Luke Gibson. When Sheriff Jerome is out of town, we're the law in Agate, so whatever you needed to see him about, you can tell us."

"I suppose that I could . . . but I won't," Longarm told them. "How far away is his mine?"

"Four or five miles. To damn far to walk."

Longarm turned and started to leave. "I'll rent a horse and ride up to see him."

"Might be a bad idea. Guards are posted on the road as well as no-trespassing signs."

"Thanks for the warning," Longarm told the deputies as he headed back outside.

He lit the cigar and studied the town. Spotting a livery, he walked on down to it, and paused beside a corral holding four saddle horses. Longarm was not one who preferred to spend a lot of time in the saddle, but he was a fair horseman and excellent judge of horseflesh. He sized the horses up, and liked the looks of a big black gelding with four white stockings.

"Interested in buying a horse?" a man behind him asked.

Longarm turned to see a smallish fella in his sixties with a wild shock of silver hair and beard to match. "Are you the proprietor?"

"I just manage this place. Jesse Jerome owns it along with most everything else in Agate. What can I do for you today?"

"I need to rent a horse."

"Going far?"

"I'm going out to the mine to see Jesse."

"You mean Mr. Jerome?"

"That's right. He and I are old friends on a first-name basis."

"For a fact," the liveryman said, eying Longarm with increased interest. "You've known him a long time, have you?"

"We go back quite a ways."

"Okay. Well, seeing as how you and Mr. Jerome are old friends, I'd better let you have my best horse and saddle and at a good rate . . . otherwise Mr. Jerome might get upset with me and I don't want that to happen."

"I like the black."

"I'm afraid that horse is owned by Mrs. Ballou. She boards it here and uses him for short rides in the countryside and when she needs to go off to Prescott."

"Then I suppose Mr. Ballou owns one of these other horses?"

"There ain't no more Mr. Ballou. He recently died quite suddenly of unknown causes."

"Is that a fact?"

"Yep. He was fit as a fiddle one day and dead as a doorknob the next. Nobody knows what happened to him exactly, and we're too small a town to have a doctor. One came, but he didn't stay long. Left just before the territorial governor was stung to death by scorpions. We gave Mr. Ballou a real nice burial. One of the best we've had so far . . . other than the one that was given to the late governor, poor feller."

"I see." Longarm turned his attention back to the corral. "What about the other three horses?"

"I'd recommend you rent the sorrel," the liveryman said. "He's a good sound animal. Got some age on him, but so do I and it ain't all bad. He's sound, he won't try to bite or kick you, and he walks right out at a good pace. He's the best riding horse in there other than that black, which is pretty high-spirited."

"Mrs. Ballou likes a high-spirited horse?"

"She sure does! She mounts that black gelding and away they go flying out of town as if the devil was hot on their tail. She's quite a horsewoman. Her husband didn't care much for horses, but Mrs. Ballou goes riding at least every couple of days."

"Where does she go?"

"Ain't none of my business," the liveryman said, his smile dying. "Ain't anybody's business, I'd say."

"All right," Longarm said. "I'll rent the sorrel. How much?"

"A dollar a day, which includes the tack."

"Saddle him up."

Longarm rode up the main street fifteen minutes later, and damned if Mrs. Ballou wasn't standing in the doorway of the Agate Hotel. He tipped his hat to her and she nodded, but didn't offer him a smile as he rode out of Agate heading for Jesse Jerome's gold mine.

Longarm had no trouble finding the Jerome Mine because of the many ore wagons he met. But about a half mile from the actual mine itself, he was stopped by a rifle-toting guard.

"Hold up there!" the bearded man shouted. "State your name and business."

"United States Deputy Marshal Custis Long. I came here to see Jesse, who's an old friend."

The guard didn't quite know how to react to this news. "You got any identification?"

Longarm pulled his coat aside and exposed his badge.

The guard stared, then stammered, "You here on official business . . . or what?"

"I don't think that's any of your concern. Now, lower that rifle and let me pass."

It was clear that the guard was confused and unsure of how to handle this unexpected situation. "I . . . I got to find out if it's all right to let you pass or not."

Longarm took a deep breath. He supposed he could have drawn his side arm and gotten the drop on this man, but the guard was such a mule-headed fool that he might actually try to shoot it out. Figuring that a few minutes' delay was better than having to shoot the guard, Longarm

41

said, "I'll wait while you go tell your boss that I'm here."

"You promise?"

Longarm almost laughed, but managed to keep a straight face and dip his chin in agreement.

"All right then. I'll be right back!"

The guard had a swaybacked pinto tied to a bush close by, and he mounted, then galloped up the dirt road to the office, which was at the end of a small canyon and shaded by trees. Longarm relaxed and waited, noting that there was a lot of activity going on at the mining claim. He could see a steady procession of workers pushing wheelbarrows out of the mine and dumping them in a pile, which was then shoveled into waiting ore wagons. Longarm could see at least thirty men at work, and that didn't include the ones in the mine itself.

Must be pretty high-grade ore if they're loading all of it for a smelter, he thought as he lit a cigar and cocked one knee around his saddle horn while waiting. *Jerome must be doing well indeed.*

Longarm recalled that Jesse had always had tastes that had far outstripped his small federal salary. That was why he'd also been a gambler, hoping for the one big poker hand that would win him what he considered his rightful due.

It appeared that had finally happened. And now that it obviously had, Longarm wondered if Jesse was content to be merely rich . . . or if unbridled greed had transformed him into a killer with political ambitions.

Longarm's dark ruminations were interrupted when he saw Jesse burst out of the mining shack. His old friend mounted the guard's horse, then came galloping out to the property boundary with a wide smile on his handsome face. Longarm was struck by how well Jesse had aged. The man had to be in his mid-forties, but he rode ramrod straight and tall in the saddle. His face had a few more lines, but he was still a striking figure and fine specimen of manhood.

"Custis Long!" Jesse shouted as he drew the already

winded pinto up and then rode in close with an outstretched hand. "Sure is good to see you after so many years. And I hear that you're still working for the government."

"Yep," Longarm said, shaking his old friend's hand, which was now soft but still able to exert a powerful grip. "Still just a deputy marshal. But Billy Vail is a full marshal. He rides a desk chair now and has a fine family. He told me to say hello and to give you his best."

"By gawd, Billy and me, we had some good times and bad together! Does he still look about the same?"

"Heavier, but otherwise the same."

Jesse patted a small but noticeable paunch. "We all get a little softer with age," he said. "But you still look rock-hard. Even a bit leaner than I remember. The feds must be working you too hard."

"They keep me on the go."

"I'll bet they do. You and Billy were the only ones beside myself worth their salt when I left the agency. And I'll bet they've still got more than their fail share of dead-wood."

"I wouldn't want to admit that you're right." Longarm motioned toward the mine. "It looks like you finally struck the big bonanza."

"I did! If the biggest gold vein holds up, I'm going to be richer than a damned railroad baron! And the good part is that I didn't have to skin anyone in the process of making my fortune."

"That's great. You always said that you'd get rich someday, and now you're doing it. I'm happy for you."

"What about yourself, Custis? Why is a man of your caliber still making peanuts working for the feds? I always thought you'd do right well yourself."

"I'm happy enough with what I do and who I am," Longarm replied, trying to sound satisfied with his lot in life.

"Ah, hell!" Jesse scoffed. "That's entirely the wrong attitude. You have to believe that you deserve the finest,

43

otherwise you'll never have anything. Why, if I'd had a satisfied mind when I was teaching you the ropes, I'd still be an underpaid, overworked federal lawman."

"I expect so."

Jesse reached into his tailored jacket and extracted two long, black cigars. "Get rid of that piece of shit you're smoking and try one of these. They're Cuban Masters. Best cigars that money can buy."

Longarm curbed the impulse to tell his old friend that his cheap little stogies suited him just fine. He didn't need to smoke expensive cigars that were as long as carrots, but he didn't want to insult Jesse, so he did as he was asked.

"Here," Jesse said, clipping ends off both cigars with small silver scissors. "When you smoke one of these, you'll never want to touch—let alone smoke—another cheap cheroot again."

They lit up and smoked for several minutes. Longarm had to admit that the Cuban cigar was one of the finest he'd ever had the pleasure of enjoying. After several minutes, Jesse said, "Custis, what brings you to our fair community of Agate?"

"Maybe I'm just passing through and I heard about your sudden wealth and wanted to stop by and congratulate you."

Jesse chuckled. "Now, I sure do wish I could believe that. Yes, sir, I really do. But the truth is, you're just a dog on a federal leash. You go when and where they tell you to go and nowhere else. So let's not bullshit each other. You're here because of the Scorpion Murders. Isn't that right?"

Longarm knew that it was pointless to deny the fact to his old mentor, so he nodded, deciding to let Jesse talk. Jesse had always preferred the sound of his own voice to that of any other. If you let him go on, he was just as likely as not to tell you things that were of real interest.

"Well, then," Jesse said, dismounting and tying the pinto up as his guard hurried out on foot to join them, "why don't you tie your horse up and let's take a little stroll down by the creek. We can sit in the shade, smoke, and talk without being overheard by my own people, who I'm sure are just dying to know the nature of your unexpected visit."

"Sounds good," Longarm agreed.

"Buster," Jesse said to the puffing guard who had just completed running up from the mining shack. "You can let Marshal Long come here anytime he wants. He's a friend of mine who can always be trusted."

"Yes, sir!"

"We've got nothing to hide, remember?" Jesse said as if lecturing a dull schoolchild. "We're a law-abiding and legitimate gold and silver mine and we're not hiding anything. Remember how I explained that to you a couple of times before?"

Buster grinned and nodded over and over like a duck. "I sure do, Boss."

"Good. Now just watch over our horses while my old friend and I go for a little walk."

"Mr. Jerome," Buster said, grabbing up his rifle. "Don't you think I ought to come along? Might be that someone—"

"We're fine!" Jesse snapped. "Custis and I could stand off a small army of assassins."

"Yes, sir."

As Jesse walked away he muttered under his breath, "Buster is a little thick between the ears, but he's a good man. He tries hard and, most importantly, he's loyal. And these days, loyalty is one of the qualities that I most value."

As they walked toward a line of trees that fed on a stream, Longarm asked, "Are you in some kind of danger?"

Jesse took a few strides, then turned and smoked for a moment. "When a man gets rich and powerful, he creates all sorts of enemies. I've tried to do right by those I've

45

dealt with since coming into money . . . but you never know who holds a grudge or resentment in the dark silence of their hearts. A man might smile and say all the right things and you might even consider him a true friend . . . until he puts a bullet in your back."

"That sounds pretty hard, Jesse."

"Life is hard. I always told you that, but I'm not sure you ever fully believed me. Do you still have that old streak of idealism? The belief that you are always doing what is just and right?"

Longarm didn't like to be talked down to, and he didn't like Jesse's air of superiority, but he managed to hide his resentment and say, "I still operate by the book, Jesse. I know what the law says and I try to follow it. I don't pretend that I'm anything but a low-paid federal marshal."

Jesse made a face. "What a crock! Damn, Custis, when are you going to wake up to reality! The law isn't made to protect the innocent . . . it's made for criminals to abuse. What happens when you bring in some murdering, raping sonofabitch to the judge?"

Before Longarm could answer, Jesse rushed on. "I'll tell you what happens. If he can get his hands on some money and hires a good attorney, he most likely will get off with his life and then an early parole on good behavior! It used to make my guts churn to see men that I risked my life to catch thumb their noses at the law and either go scot-free or get a pat on the wrist and be out on parole in a couple of years to commit the same damn crime . . . if not one even worse."

"That's in the past, Jesse. I'm not here to argue about the merits or failures of our justice system. You had your way of dealing with fugitives and I've got mine. So let's move on or we're both going to get angry and maybe say something that we regret."

Jesse took a deep breath and let his broad shoulders settle. "You're right, Custis. We're friends and I hope that

46

we always will be. So let's talk about why you are here and what you want from me."

They entered the shady area under the big water-loving trees. Longarm chose a rock to sit down upon and Jesse took another. It was cool and the stream was clear. There were ferns and a dark, deep pool of water that would make a good swimming or fishing hole.

"Any fish in there?" Longarm asked after they had smoked for several minutes in silence.

"Hell, I don't know! You were the one that liked to fish and eat trout. I never had the patience for fishing, and I'd much rather eat steak than fish any old day."

"Yeah," Longarm said, remembering. "So tell me how you came to own this rich mine."

"Haven't you heard the story yet?"

"I have, but I'd like to hear your version."

"I won it playing cards. The man who owned it previously was actually an even better poker player than myself, and had won far more money from me over a period of several months than I'd taken off him. But on the particular night that I won this mine, I was on an unbelievable roll of good luck. I couldn't believe the hands I was being dealt, and my luck just held and held until I'd taken him for everything he owned or ever would own."

"Were there any witnesses?"

"Hell, yes! You want their names?" Jesse's cheeks flushed with anger. "Are you here to try and decide if I came into ownership of the mine by other than honest means?"

"Take it easy. I just have to ask the questions. Don't you remember how it works?"

Jesse relaxed a bit, but now he smoked fast. "All right. I remember. And I know you are here to do your job and that the job counts more than any old friendship."

"Jesse, that ain't fair."

"But it's true."

Longarm couldn't deny the fact, but said, "Billy decided to send someone else to investigate the Scorpion Murders. He even told me straight out that he was afraid that our friendship would muddy my mind and that I'd be incapable of doing a fair or thorough investigation."

"Billy said that to you?"

"That's right. But I told him I'd abide by the law and do whatever had to be done."

"Meaning try to arrest me if you thought I was guilty of murder."

"Yes," Longarm said, looking the man squarely in the eyes so that there would be no misunderstanding of his intentions.

"And do you think I'm capable of murder . . . using scorpions, for crying out loud?"

Longarm didn't answer the question directly. "I only remember that I've seen you kill quite a few men."

"But always in the line of duty. Always men who *deserved* to die. Always just the dregs of the earth. Human scum. That's the kind of men that you saw me try to arrest, then be forced to kill."

"Sometimes," Longarm said, choosing his words carefully, "maybe you *weren't* forced to kill them."

Jesse jumped to his feet. "I see. Apparently, you shared the opinion of the department when they accused me of taking the law into my own hands and firing me."

"That's not true."

"Oh?"

"They asked me to write an account of all the times I saw you shoot someone down. I flatly refused. I told them that, in my opinion, you never killed anyone unless there was no choice."

"Is that what you *really* told them?" Jesse challenged.

"I just said it was."

"Then why was I fired?"

"Maybe there were some that said otherwise." Longarm stood up. "Are we moving against each other here, Jesse? Or can we work this out so that I can go back to Denver telling Billy and anyone else that asks that you won this mine fair and square and that I found and arrested the real Scorpion Murderer?"

"I'm innocent."

"Prove it!"

"No," Jesse said. "The law and the Constitution says that a man is innocent until proven guilty. So, my old friend, it's going to be *your* job to get the proof necessary to clear my good name and reputation. I'm a rich and free man now, and I'll be damned if I'll waste my valuable time trying to prove something that I already know."

"So that's it?" Longarm asked.

"That's it."

"Then I'll do my best, but I'm still going to need help."

"I can't help you," Jesse said flatly.

Longarm's voice took on an edge. "Why not?"

"Because anything that I might say in my own behalf would only be questioned. So you'll have to find the proof of my innocence all by yourself."

"That's not what I'd hoped to hear from you," Longarm said, exhaling a cloud of blue smoke. "You're making this even harder than I'd expected it to be."

"I'm sorry."

Longarm was exasperated. "Can't you at least tell me the names of the witnesses that saw you win your gold mine?"

"They're all either dead or they drifted away."

"Give me some names!"

"All right. Let's go to my office and I'll write them down on paper. Who knows? Maybe one or two are still alive and living in Arizona someplace and can be located."

"I hope so," Longarm said. "It would be a good start."

"Meaning that, even if you do find witnesses to collaborate what I've just told you about winning the mine fair and square, you'll then move on to investigate if I'm responsible for the Scorpion Murders?"

"That's right."

49

Jesse Jerome shook his head. "When you start asking people about me, most will declare without a shred of proof that I'm the one that killed the governor and that miserable little toad who called himself a newspaper reporter. I'll bet nine out of ten folks that you question will say that Jesse Jerome is as guilty as the day is long."

"So who would be the one in ten who would say you are innocent?"

"Buster believes I'm innocent."

"He probably still believes in Santa Claus. Who else?"

Jesse laughed, then said, "The liveryman who rented you a horse doesn't think I'm guilty of any crime."

"That's not good enough," Longarm said, "because he admitted that you own the livery and he's on your payroll. That makes his word suspect."

"Then how about you ask Mrs. Delia Ballou?"

Longarm exhaled a cloud of smoke. "You don't own a stake in her hotel, do you?"

"Not yet."

"But you're hoping to?"

"I'm hoping," Jesse said slowly, "to own Delia before much longer. And by that I mean . . . to make her my wife."

"You don't *own* a wife, Jesse. Or haven't you moved into the modern age of individual freedom?"

"Just a figure of speech, my friend. That's all."

Longarm wasn't so sure. He well remembered the exploits of this man when it came to women. Jesse had always been a lady-killer, and he'd left a string of broken hearts all over the West. He'd loved them and left them without a moment's hesitation or a twinge of a guilty conscience. He might have changed his attitude toward the fairer sex . . . but Longarm rather doubted it.

"Let's go to your offices and we'll get some names," Longarm said.

"Good idea," the former lawman quipped, removing his hat and running his fingers through his thick hair. "I'm glad I thought of it."

Chapter 6

Longarm got a lot of curious stares from the employees both inside and outside the mining office. The moment they entered the office, Jesse bellowed, "Everyone, I want you meet my old lawman friend United States Deputy Marshal Custis Long. Custis and I put some bad men in prison and we put a hell of a lot more in the ground!"

There was nervous laughter at this poor attempt at humor, and then Jesse ushered Longarm into his private office and shut the door. The office was—to put it mildly—opulent and completely unexpected for something way out in the mountains. The oak floors were partially covered with fine Oriental rugs, and the magnificent cherrywood desk would have befitted a United States senator. There was a huge oil painting of Jesse Jerome, with an ornate frame that glittered with what Longarm supposed was real gold dust. In the portrait, Jesse was standing with his hand resting on a pearl-handled revolver at his hip, the same one he was wearing now.

"Not bad, huh?" Jesse said, collapsing in his office chair and lacing his fingers behind his head as he gazed with satisfaction at his surroundings.

"Not bad at all," Longarm agreed. "This is quite a little setup you have out here."

"Nothing little about it, Custis. We ship a very high grade of both gold and silver ore to a smelter I own about eight miles to the north. I can't tell you what the assay numbers are, but they'd make any mining man drool with envy."

"So when are you going to run for governor?"

"Oh, you heard about that already?"

"Of course. That was kind of an unusual way for the former territorial governor to die, wouldn't you admit?"

"Stanton was a worthless and corrupt windbag, though I usually refrain from speaking ill of the dead."

"Since you didn't kill him, who do you suppose did?" Longarm asked.

Jesse shrugged. "Hell, I don't know, but the fella ought to be awarded a medal. He did Arizona a big, big favor."

"You got any proof of the former governor's graft?"

"No. Besides, what does it matter to you? You're only interested in who killed Governor Stanton, not why he was killed."

"One question," Longarm said, "ties directly to the other."

"I suppose. Governor Stanton had a lot of enemies, and I'll admit that I was high on that list. We disagreed on almost everything, and when he tried to raise mining fees and drain me of my rightful profits, I naturally objected."

"Why do you suppose Stanton was doused in his sleep by a bunch of especially poisonous scorpions?"

"I have no idea."

"Scorpions aren't usually fatal, are they?"

"Nope. But the kind that were used on the governor and that reporter were kinda special."

"Meaning?"

"Meaning that they're only found deep in the heart of the Sonoran Desert. Where it's hottest and every living thing has spikes, claws, or teeth and whatever is poison

52

is twice the poison that is found anyplace else in this hard country."

"I see." Longarm was still working on the Cuban cigar. "So what happened to the scorpions used to kill the reporter and the governor?"

"Damned if I know."

"They were destroyed, weren't they?"

"I have no idea. I heard that no one even wanted to go into those hotel rooms. Poor Delia had to kill them herself, though I'd have done it for her if I'd known that all the men in Agate had all suddenly became cowards."

"What do you suppose killed her husband?"

"Again, I have no idea or interest. He wasn't a strong man. He'd once been a professor at some Eastern college. He'd come out for his health, met Delia, and you'll have to ask her why she married such a weakling."

"He must have had something going in his favor to attract such a beautiful woman," Longarm suggested.

Jesse's eyes narrowed. "If you can tell me the answer to why some women see something special in weak men, I'd like to know. But if pressed for an answer, I suppose Delia's head might have been turned by his learning. Homer Ballou was a very educated man. He could—and did—spout poetry. Lots of it, but mainly Shakespeare. I found him to be a complete boor. He was very impressed with himself, and I always thought he considered himself a big cut above us Western men. And he had some money and family background. He's the one that bought the Agate Hotel, but he only did it because Delia hounded him into making the purchase."

Longarm heard envy and bitterness in his old friend's voice. Jesse was nearly old enough to be Mrs. Ballou's father, but that wouldn't stop him from wanting her anyway.

"Mrs. Ballou owns a very spirited horse, which I was told she likes to ride at least a couple of times a week."

"So?"

"Any idea where she goes?"

"Of course not! What difference would it make anyway?"

"I was just wondering if she might be meeting another man," Longarm said as casually as possible.

Longarm got the eruption he'd expected. "What the hell are you talking about?" Jesse shouted. "Delia is going to marry me!"

"Is she aware of that fact?"

Jesse reached up, tore his cigar from his teeth, and stabbed it into an ashtray. "Custis," he hissed, "if you weren't my friend, I'd probably smash your face in right now."

"Then I'm glad that we're friends because that kind of thing would really make me mad and I'd have to kick your butt up between your ears."

"You think you're man enough to do that?"

Longarm set his own cigar in the ashtray. "I don't see any point in us talking anymore right now. I'm going to start talking to the locals and I'll get back to you soon."

"I'll be here."

"I'm sure that you will."

"Lock your door at night when you go to bed," Jesse warned. "I wouldn't want you to suffer the same fate as the governor and that weasel of a reporter. And I wouldn't want you to be roaming around the hotel and maybe open the wrong door."

"Meaning the one to Mrs. Ballou's bedroom?" Longarm dared ask.

"Exactly. She's mine, Custis. If I found out that you were interested in her for any reason other than your investigation, I'd take it very badly."

"I see."

"I do mean to marry her."

"Yes. And *own* her, if I recall your exact word."

"Get out of here before I throw you out."

"I'm on my way. Are you going to change your instructions to Buster about letting me come and go whenever I want?"

"I don't know yet. But I'm thinking that I might."

"Don't," Longarm warned. "If you become inaccessible, then I might start thinking you are trying to hide something from me. Something very important."

"I'll give you five seconds to leave this office and then I'm going to throw you the hell out!"

Longarm turned and left, and damned if he couldn't hear Jesse Jerome starting to count. The man hadn't changed even a little bit despite all his newfound wealth. He still possessed a murderous temper, and it could explode at any given moment with even the slightest provocation.

"He isn't guilty," a rough miner said as Longarm walked across the busy yard and out to the gate where his horse waited beside Buster. "Mr. Jerome isn't the Scorpion Killer."

Longarm paused in mid-stride. "Do you have any proof that you can offer to back up your claim?"

"I just know that if he had killed the governor and that reporter, he'd have walked right up, gave them the order to go for their own weapons, then shot them both in the guts."

"I hope you're right."

"He told everyone in the office you were his friend. I don't think you are anymore, Marshal."

"You're wrong about that," Longarm told the big miner, who had a massive jaw and whose fists were clenched. "I'm still Jesse's friend, but maybe the feeling isn't mutual anymore."

"I wouldn't come back here if I was you."

"You're not me," Longarm told the man. "So step aside."

The miner held his ground. "Maybe you ought to walk around, Marshal."

"I told you to step aside."

"Go to hell," the miner growled as he drove his fist up in a tight arc between them.

Longarm had read the man's intent in his deep-set eyes, and he twisted, causing the big miner to punch his holstered gun. It must have hurt because the man grunted with pain, and before he could recover, Longarm stomped his heel down hard on the miner's boot, then stepped back and kicked him right between his legs hard enough to lift him to his toes.

The miner's eyes dilated with pain. He groaned and grabbed for his crotch, and Longarm brought his own uppercut up to connect with that heavy jaw. It felt as if he'd punched a tree, but the miner went down hard and he didn't get up, but instead clutched his genitals and cried like a baby.

"Nice touch," Jesse said, coming up behind Longarm. "Now why don't you get off this property before I show you what a real man can do with his fists."

"You don't want to do that," Longarm said. "Besides, you taught me most of your fighting skills. Remember?"

"Yeah. I remember."

"I'll give your best to Mrs. Ballou when I get back to town. See you around, Jesse."

"You sonofabitch!"

Longarm ducked an overhand right and spun around to face his old friend and mentor. "You've slowed, Jesse. Now why don't you go back to that pretty office before you make a fool of yourself?"

Jesse quivered, and Longarm could see how badly he wanted to wade in swinging. But he'd never been stupid, and with dozens of men watching them, he couldn't have stood the humiliation of getting whipped. So he relaxed, and even managed to pull off a frozen smile.

"Custis, get out of here," he said in a low voice. "I don't think you're my friend anymore."

"That's what the one on the ground said and look what happened to him," Longarm replied. "I'm still your friend,

Jesse. But if you're really innocent, then you've got to help me prove it."

"*You* prove it. That's your job, not mine."

"Oh yes. I'd forgotten," Longarm answered. "Your time is now far too valuable to show an old friend the truth."

Jesse Jerome didn't have a reply, so Longarm went out to his horse. He took the reins from Buster, who was glaring at him with hot, angry eyes.

"You got something to say to me, Buster?"

"Yeah. You ain't a friend of Mr. Jerome. And you shouldn't ever come back here again."

"Don't make the mistake of trying to stop me if I do," Longarm warned. "Being stupid is no excuse for getting yourself either hurt or in serious trouble."

Then Longarm tore the reins from Buster's clenched fist and mounted the sorrel. He rode off feeling the hateful stares of everyone at the Jerome Mine, including those of its owner.

When he returned to Agate, he felt drained and sad. The meeting out at the mine had gone worse than he could have imagined.

"Marshal," the liveryman said, "you look pretty unhappy."

"I am. What is your name?"

"Gus."

"Well, Gus. I thought that Jesse Jerome was my friend, but he sure didn't act like one today."

"He has an awful bad temper. Maybe you said something that made him mad."

"Yeah," Longarm agreed. "I think I said a lot of things that made him mad."

"You shouldn't do that."

"Why?"

Gus toed the dirt with his worn, round-toed boot. " 'Cause a man could get in bad trouble by making Mr. Jerome mad. Real bad trouble."

"You mean he'd try to kill me?"

"Oh, no! Not that, but he'd do his best to make sure that you left town."

"And how would he go about doing that?"

"I guess he'd make sure you couldn't find work and that when you walked into a saloon, you'd probably come out feet first and not feeling none too good."

"I see."

"What did you think of the horse?"

"He's a good one. Walks right out and isn't a bit spooky, even around those big ore wagons we kept passing."

"I told you that you'd like him," Gus said. "So what are you going to do now?"

"I'm going to start asking questions and trying to find out who's behind the murders."

"It ain't Mr. Jerome."

"That's what his friends keep saying, but they don't have any idea who did commit the crimes."

"That's because none of us has any idea. Oh, we talk about it all the time, but no one knows. Everyone in town has been accused, and a lot of the folks that Mr. Jerome bought out for only a few cents on the dollar sure enough would like to see him tagged with the murder charges. But he's as innocent as I am."

"And how," Longarm asked, keeping a straight face, "do I know that you're innocent?"

Gus's eyes widened and he stammered, "Why would an old used-up goat like me murder someone?"

"I don't know, but then, I don't know you very well yet."

"Well, if you did, you'd know I wouldn't hurt nobody."

Gus looked so upset that Longarm laid a hand on his skinny shoulder and said, "I believe you, old-timer. Don't worry, I'm sure that you're completely innocent of any wrongdoing. You've probably never done a single illegal act in your entire life."

Gus relaxed. "Well, I skinned a lot of folks on buyin'

and sellin' horses, and I once snitched a box of sardine cans, but I felt so bad that when I got the money, I paid the merchant back."

"You're a good man, Gus. And if you should hear anything about those murders that might help me find out who really is the guilty party, I hope that you'll tell me."

"Oh, I will. I have my theories just like everyone else in Agate, but no proof yet. Still, I'm working on it in my own slow, quiet way."

"You want to tell me who you suspect?"

"Rather not, Marshal. But I will if I figure it out for sure."

"Thanks," Longarm said before heading back to the Agate Hotel.

Chapter 7

Delia was sitting in the hotel lobby all by herself when Longarm tromped in and headed for the stairs.

"Did you have a good visit with your old friend?" she called out.

Longarm stopped and came back to sit down in an overstuffed chair across from the hotel owner. Delia was wearing a long pink and white checkered dress. Her black hair was pulled back and tied by a scarf and draped over one shoulder. She looked so lovely that Custis had to take a deep breath before he remembered to answer her question.

"I'm afraid not. It started out all right, but Jesse lost his temper and wound up throwing a punch at me."

Her eyes widened. "Did you hurt him?"

"No. I stepped back and then walked away. But I wasn't invited back to the mine."

Delia shook her head. "Jesse's temper is well known in these parts. How long ago was it when you knew him?"

"About ten years. He hasn't changed one bit except that he's a little older."

"And much richer but not wiser."

"You said that. I didn't."

"Were you pretty close friends at one time?"

"Yeah. Jesse took me under his wing when I became a federal marshal, and he taught me what I needed to know in order to stay alive and do my job. He saved my life— not once, but twice."

"Then you owe him a great deal."

"That's for sure."

"Why didn't you demand that someone else come from Denver in your place? There must have been another marshal who could have come to Agate without any obligations due to an old and valued friendship."

"There were," Longarm admitted. "And after what happened today out at the mine, I realize that I was wrong to come here. But I had hoped that my friendship with Jesse would somehow allow me to unlock the mystery of who really killed the former governor and that newspaper reporter. I was convinced that Jesse couldn't have committed those crimes."

"And do you still feel that way?"

Longarm heaved a deep sigh. "I'm not so sure anymore. Jesse looked me straight in the eye and said he was innocent . . . but at the same time he refused to give me any help at all as to who might be the guilty party."

"So you are beginning to question his innocence."

"Yes." Longarm removed his hat and ran his fingers through his hair. "It seems to me that if he were innocent, he would at least try to help me find the true killer. Especially since he is the prime suspect."

Delia leaned closer, hands clasped together in her lap. "Why is Jesse the prime suspect?"

"I think you can guess the reasons. He's the one that wound up with ownership of the gold mine and half this town. Speaking of which, does anyone know what happened to the former mine owner?"

"He left Agate the night he lost his fortune. He's never been seen again."

"What was his name?"

"Mike Kelly. He was a gambler and he could deal off the bottom of the deck better than any man I've ever seen."

"Do you think he's still alive?"

"As far as I know he is. Why do you ask?"

"I'd like to hear his version of what happened the night he lost his mine."

"I knew Mike well. If you asked him that question, he would just say that his luck went bad and his only mistake was in not walking away from the table the night he was playing Jesse."

"So you don't think that he was murdered?"

"No!" Delia acted surprised by the question. "Why should he have been murdered if he had nothing left?"

"I don't know," Longarm replied. "But it would help if I knew that Jesse really did win that gold mine in an honest poker game."

Delia almost laughed. "Marshal, you must know that most games are dishonest. It's a matter of *who* is cheating, not *if* someone is cheating. I will say this. Jesse is not a card cheat. I've never heard anyone accuse him of double dealing or having a card up his sleeve or any such thing. And frankly, I don't think Jesse is the kind of man whose pride would allow him to cheat. That's why he always lost to the professionals like Mike Kelly. And why, on the night he had his phenomenal streak of luck, he somehow managed to beat a man who was dealing cards off the bottom. Don't you see how remarkable it was that an honest and lesser card player beat a better and dishonest one?"

"Yes, I do. But I'd still like to talk to Mike Kelly."

"He wouldn't tell you anything. My guess is he's long gone, and probably cheating someone at a game of cards even as we speak."

"Tell me about the deaths of the territorial governor and the reporter."

Delia took a deep breath. "You're asking quite a lot. I

63

think that you should at least buy me a drink and dinner."

"I'd be happy. . . ." Longarm paused.

"What?" she asked.

"Jesse was pretty clear about the fact that he intends to marry you and that I had better keep things between us strictly business."

Delia shook her head. "Jesse wants everything that he can't have. He wants my hotel and he wants me, but I'm not for sale and neither is this hotel."

"But you offered to sell it to me the first time I walked in here."

"That's because I'll sell it to anyone other than Jesse Jerome. My heavens, he's already strangled Agate! He owns most of the buildings and he charges such high rents that everyone is in danger of going out of business."

"That doesn't make much sense."

"Jesse Jerome almost never makes sense," Delia said. "And now that he is rich and powerful, his ambition and greed are boundless. No, I won't sell to him. I'd rather starve first!"

"Then I take it you've no intention of marrying the man."

"That's right."

- "He doesn't realize that fact."

"Of course not. The more emphatic I am about not ever marrying Jesse, the more determined he becomes. I've become his obsession, and believe me, I find that very frightening."

Longarm shook his head and decided not to tell her about Jesse's remark that one day he'd "own" her. "So why don't you just close up and leave Agate? Surely you can't survive if I'm the only boarder you have?"

"Others come and go. I do just enough business to stay alive. And I keep hoping that someday, some tall, rugged, and handsome man like yourself who loves this part of the country and this hotel will make me a reasonable offer. Either that, or Jesse will lose his temper once too often and be killed."

Longarm figured that his face must have betrayed his shock at her words, because Delia quickly added, "I know that sounded terrible. And I really don't want Jesse to be killed, but he has almost killed this town and every day he is becoming more ruthless and bold. Something has to give, and I don't want it to be me. Is that so awful?"

"I suppose not," Longarm said. "But it did catch me by surprise."

"There's a cafe just up the street owned by a friend of mine who has also resisted being bought out by Jesse. Why don't we go there and have something to eat? We can get a table in the back part of the room and talk without being overheard or disturbed by any of Jesse's miners or cronies."

"Why? Did they also blackball your friend's cafe?"

"As a matter of fact, they did."

"And how does he stay in business?"

"He's hanging on by a thread."

"All right," Longarm said, knowing that people would start talking the moment they stepped outside and walked down the street. And that what they saw and heard would be blown all out of proportion, and it would reach Jesse, who would be enraged.

To hell with it, Longarm thought. *It's a free country and, if I want, I can have a drink and supper with this woman.*

Delia locked the hotel up and he offered her his arm. Then, they strolled past the empty shops and businesses and gawking onlookers down to the Ponderosa Cafe, owned by a pleasant-looking man in his mid-thirties named Hank Walton.

"Good afternoon," Walton said, standing in front of his counter. "As you can see, any table in the place is yours for the asking."

"We'll sit in the back corner," Delia told her friend.

65

"Hank, this is Marshal Custis Long from Denver. He's here to investigate the Scorpion Murders."

"You aren't the first. Jesse Jerome himself claimed to have done an investigation, but said that the killer or killers must have run away and can't be found."

"I hope to come up with something different," Longarm said. "I hope to prove or disprove that Jesse was behind the killings."

"Good luck."

"Hank, could you bring us a bottle of my favorite wine? Unless you'd rather have some beer or whiskey," Delia quickly added, looking at Custis.

"Wine is good with a steak. How about steaks for dinner?"

"Both of you?" the cafe owner asked.

"Fine," Delia told him as she led the way back to a corner table. As soon as they were seated and the wine was poured, Delia raised her glass in salute. "To your success and long life, Marshal."

Custis paused, then smiled and matched the toast. They drank and then eased back into their chairs a moment before Longarm said, "Now how about telling me exactly what happened to the former territorial governor and that reporter?"

"All right. The governor got drunk and went to bed. He was actually quite a pig. In the morning, when he didn't come down for breakfast, I went upstairs and banged on his door. He didn't answer and I finally had to use the hotel's room key. When I opened the door . . ."

Delia halted, then drained her glass and continued. "When I opened the door, the man was crawling with scorpions. They were all over him and the bed. I screamed and slammed the door for a moment. Then I took a deep breath and went to get a heavy broom. I rushed back inside, opened the window shades, and let sunlight into the room. Then I smashed them as they scuttled around trying

66

to get away. I swept them out from under the bed and killed every last one."

"At quite a risk to yourself!"

"Not really," Delia said. "Scorpions are night creatures. In broad daylight, they seek darkness. I've seen plenty of scorpions, but these were darker and bigger than the locals. All they really wanted to do was to get away."

"Do you know if there were any other signs of violence committed on the governor other than the scorpion stings?"

"You mean, did I see a bullet hole or a knife wound?"

"Exactly."

"No, I didn't. Only the places where the scorpions had stung him, and that was bad enough."

"What about the reporter? He was probably younger and stronger, but I understand someone tied him spread-eagled to the bed."

"Would you refill my glass, please?"

"Of course," Longarm said.

"The reporter had been tied to the bedposts. A gag had been stuffed halfway down his throat, and I'll never forget the horror I saw stamped on his poor swollen and purplish face."

Delia shuddered, took a drink, and continued the gruesome account. "That death was even uglier to witness than the death of the governor. At least Stanton had died drunk and might not even have known he was being stung to death. But the reporter had obviously died in a most hideous and horrible manner. He'd expired slowly and in extreme agony. It might have taken several hours for the venom to have finally done its complete and deadly work."

Delia drained her second glass of wine. She looked up at Longarm and said, "I appear to be on the way to getting tipsy. And I'm drinking all the wine. I apologize."

"We'll get another bottle. I'm paying. I don't mind. But

I do need to ask again if there were any other signs of physical violence on the reporter."

"Actually, there were. He had been beaten about the head. There was dried blood in his scalp and his face was cut where someone had either used their fists or a heavy object."

"And you found him in the morning, just like with the former governor?"

"That's right. Same thing exactly. When he didn't show up the next morning, I went up to his room, stood outside his door, and knocked. No answer, so I called and called. By the time I used my own house key to open his door, my hands were shaking badly because I had a premonition about what had happened. And my worst fears were realized. His body was smaller, but there were just as many scorpions crawling on his bed. Once again, I rushed to open the window shade and they all tried to flee. I got my broom and beat them to a pulp."

"Same kind of scorpions?"

"Exactly the same. My heavens, if I ever see one on my bed, I'll probably just die of fright!"

"I somehow doubt that," Longarm told her. "You strike me as being a very strong woman. And I'm sorry that you lost your husband."

"Homer was a good man," Delia said. "However, he didn't really fit here in Agate. I know that Jesse and a lot of men wondered why I married Homer. The truth was, he was kind, gentle, and a very decent fellow. He had a wonderful sense of humor and made me laugh. And laughter, in this town, is a very scare commodity."

"And no idea at all why he died?"

"Homer had a family history of heart problems," Delia explained. "He would wake up in the night beside me drenched in sweat and breathing so hard that I could almost hear his hammering heart. He'd had several bad moments with chest pains. I think his heart just quit."

Delia's eyes filled with tears, and she emptied the bottle

into her water glass and tossed it all down in several swallows. "Oh, I do miss Homer! He was a fine man. A scholar and a gentleman. He was just the complete opposite of Jesse Jerome."

Longarm signaled Hank to bring them more wine. When it arrived, the cafe owner said, "Delia, are you all right?"

"I'll be fine," she managed to whisper. "But give the marshal and me some time before you bring those steaks."

"Sure thing. Marshal, maybe you'd rather have whiskey?"

"As a matter of fact I would," Longarm said, studying the beautiful woman across from him. "Bring a bottle over. This has been a hard day for both the lady and myself."

"Okay."

It was several minutes before Delia felt like talking again, and it was obvious that she was trying hard to recover her composure. "So," she said, "enough of this scorpion business. Marshal Long, why don't you tell me a little about yourself."

"Not much to tell really."

"I don't believe that for one minute. Where did you grow up?"

"In West Virginia."

"And then there was the terrible War Between the States?"

"Yes," Longarm said, "which I decline to talk about. The past is the past and I look more to the future."

"I wish that I had a future to look forward to," Delia said, "but right now all I see is darkness and defeat."

"It'll get better," Longarm promised. "Things get better if you don't give up on life."

"I'll try to remember that. And are you the one that is going to make them get better?"

"I don't know. Would they suddenly get better if I

prove to myself that Jesse is guilty of those murders and have to either arrest or kill him?"

"I don't know." Delia shook her head. "Despite his temper and his overbearing and ruthless way of going about things, I still don't believe he had a thing to do with those two murders. You're going to have to have some pretty substantial evidence to change my mind or to go after him. In case you haven't noticed, Jesse keeps himself well protected with his gunmen. He's got some very unsavory and rough characters on his payroll. I know that because they are not above harassing me now and then."

"In what way?"

"They'll come into my hotel and plop down on my furniture. They'll clean their boots on my lovely carpets and when I protest, laugh and leer at me, as if daring me to do anything."

"That will stop as long as I'm staying in Agate," Longarm vowed.

Delia studied him closely. "Do you really know what you are getting into here? My heavens, the chances of you successfully bucking Jesse and his crowd are slim . . . and none."

"I'm used to long odds," Longarm assured her. "This kind of setup is nothing new, except for the fact that the prime murder suspect just happens to have once been my mentor and best friend."

"But no more."

Longarm tossed down a gulp of whiskey. "I don't know what to think. Jesse lost his temper and wanted to hurt me bad out at his mine. I guess I was pretty shocked by that, but in recollection, I shouldn't have been. Jesse does things and then he often regrets them. I'm sure that is what happened today. I'll bet he's feeling bad about what happed at the Jerome Mine right now."

"Don't count on that. He might have changed, you know. And not for the better."

"I've considered that, and allowed after this afternoon

70

that he probably has changed for the worst. But I still don't believe he would ever be as devious as to use scorpions to do his dirty work."

"Neither do I," Delia said. "It isn't his style."

"So I have to find out who does have that style. I was thinking it might be the man who lost everything to Jesse and then went about setting him up to look like a murderer."

"You mean Mike Kelly?"

"That's right."

Delia frowned. "I suppose that is possible."

"But I'll never know because the gambler has disappeared."

"He might be found in Flagstaff."

Longarm was suddenly quite interested. Flagstaff was only a long one-day or an easy two-day ride. "What makes you think so?"

"Mike had a woman in Flagstaff. He got drunk once and admitted that he had even fathered a son there."

"Do you remember the woman's name or the name of the boy?"

"Sure. The woman's name was Claire. The boy's name was Liam. Mike swore that he was going to marry Claire so that he could give the boy his last name. I don't know if he ever got around to doing that, but I remember because I told him that was a very honorable thing to do. The right thing to do for the boy's sake."

"Do you remember anything else about them?"

"Such as?"

"What Claire did for a living? Or her last name, or anything at all that would help me locate her if I go racing off to Flagstaff?"

Delia frowned. "She was . . . a clerk in a dry-goods store. In fact, yes! Claire worked in her father's dry-goods store in downtown Flagstaff."

"That should make her easy to find."

"Don't you think that it's rather a long shot? I mean, even if you do find Mike—"

"I don't know," Longarm interrupted. "At the very least, he can substantiate the poker game where he lost his gold and silver mine. At the most, he might actually be the one responsible for the Scorpion Murders. Right now, Delia, I have no other leads to follow."

"I'll hate to see you go, Marshal. You give me a sense of security that is sorely needed."

"I'll be back in just a few days."

Delia reached across the table and took his hands in her own. "You won't be leaving until morning, will you?"

The question and the wanting look in her eyes caught him off guard. "No," he said, feeling the heat rise in his body. "I'll be staying tonight."

"Good," she breathed, obviously a little tipsy. "We have a lot to talk about, you and I."

"We do?"

"Oh, yes. I can tell that you're a gentle man. An intelligent man and one who knows how to treat a lady."

"And you are a lady."

"Yes," she agreed, "in the daylight."

Longarm swallowed hard. He leaned across the table, and her eyes closed softly. He realized that she wanted and probably needed to be kissed right here and now.

So he did kiss her. Gently. Tenderly.

Suddenly the window beside them exploded inward, showering them with glass. Longarm felt as if he'd been kicked in the head. He reared back in his chair, and remembered nothing more as he tumbled into a deep, dark abyss.

Chapter 8

Longarm awoke in his hotel room bed with a splitting headache. When he tried to sit up, it felt as if someone were pounding a steel wedge deep into his brain.

"Ugggh," he grunted, falling back on his pillow.

Delia was instantly at his side with a damp cloth to cool his face. "Custis, you've been shot in the head. It's a nasty wound, but it isn't fatal."

"Glad to hear that," he mumbled.

"We don't have a doctor, but Hank has sent for one in Prescott. I'm not sure if he'll come or not, but we're trying."

Longarm took a deep breath and raised his hand to touch the bandage wrapped around his head. "Is it just a crease?"

"It grazed bone and you lost quite a lot of blood before we could get it stopped. I think you'll be all right in a few days, but I'm no doctor and I'm worried about infection."

"I'm tough," he told her, feeling anything but tough. "What time of the night is it?"

"Three in the morning. I'm hopeful that Hank can get us a doctor by noon tomorrow."

"I don't need a doctor," Longarm told her. "Did you see who shot me?"

"No." Delia's eyes brimmed with tears. "I'd had too much wine to drink and I wasn't looking anywhere but at you. The gunshot caught me as much by surprise as it did you."

Longarm swore under his breath. "I'm not getting off to a very good start in Agate. First my old friend Jesse tries to knock my block off. Then someone tries to kill me."

"Maybe it's one and the same man."

"I don't know," Longarm said honestly. "But I can tell you this. I'll be going back out to the Jerome Mine in the next day or two and I'll have a few choice words for Jesse."

"That might be what he's hoping for. Custis, why don't you send a telegram off to Denver and ask for some help?"

"Not yet," he answered. "I think I'll go back to sleep now. Why don't you do the same."

"I will, but I'm so afraid now that I'll stay in here in your room, if you don't mind."

"Not at all. In fact, instead of sitting in that uncomfortable chair, why don't you lie down beside me? I'm certainly in no condition to compromise your virtue."

"Virtue doesn't concern me anymore. Survival is what I'm thinking most about."

"We'll survive."

"You almost didn't tonight. A half inch inward and you'd be a dead man."

"I got careless," Longarm admitted. "I should have never taken a seat close to an outside window. But I won't make the mistake again."

Delia came over and lay down beside him. Longarm almost asked if she had been sure to lock their door. But then, she was scared and no fool, so he figured that to be a dumb question.

74

• • •

They both slept almost until noon, when a doctor from Prescott arrived in a buggy driven by Hank Walton. Both men knocked on Longarm's door until Delia opened it.

"Delia, are you all right?" Hank asked, rushing inside.

"Yes."

Walton hurried over to Longarm with the doctor in tow. "Marshal, I see you're awake and still breathing."

"I'm fine," Longarm told the agitated cafe owner. "Stop looking so worried."

"Step aside," the doctor, a short, graying man with thick, wire-rimmed spectacles, ordered. "I've lost a lot of sleep and come a long way on a very bad road. You'd better have a serious head wound or I'm going to be furious!"

"I wouldn't want to disappoint you, Doctor."

"This is Dr. Carpenter," Walton said in the way of an introduction. "He's a fine doctor."

"And one who will charge a patient dearly if he's been called out in the middle of the night for anything less than a real emergency."

Longarm decided that Carpenter might be a fine physician, but he was certainly lacking in bedside manner. Not that it mattered to him much, but Carpenter was pretty rough in unwrapping the head bandages. Dried blood had stuck to the bandages, and the doctor took no care in making things either easy or painless.

"Uh-huh," Carpenter mused.

"Ouch!" Longarm cried. "Doc, I'm not some damned horse. Take it easy."

"You are a very lucky lawman," the doctor declared. "The bullet not only struck the skull, but actually creased it quite deeply. How much blood did you lose?"

"I have no idea."

"He lost a lot," Delia said, hovering close and giving Carpenter a hard look. "And you *are* being unnecessarily rough!"

75

Carpenter had a medical kit. He snapped it open, rummaged around for a moment or two, and then extracted a tube of ointment. "Apply this every four hours. It will reduce the chance of a brain infection. He might have some already, so just put it on like I do and no more bandaging. Open air promotes healing. Bandages breed disease and infection."

The doctor squeezed some of the black, sticky ointment out of the tube onto his thumb, then rubbed it over the wound, sending Longarm into a paralysis of pain.

"Dammit, Doc! Take it easy!"

Carpenter paid him no mind. "You will survive, but there will be a scalp deformity. A slight depression or raised scar, I'm not sure which, and where the wound is you could grow back white hair where there was black. Even so, you are a lucky, lucky man."

"I don't feel lucky."

"Better this than what happened to this woman's husband. He had a bad ticker."

"Heart failure?"

"Yes. I opened him up on the table. His heart had exploded like a Chinese firecracker. Poor man never had a chance. I think maybe he died of fright."

"What?"

"He looked scared in death. But then, that happens sometimes when a man knows he is dying."

Carpenter snapped his bag shut, stood straight, and looked at Hank Walton. "Twenty dollars, and you can take me back to Prescott right now."

"Doc, I'm sorry but I can't afford to pay you but half of your fee right now. Maybe . . ."

"Hold on," Longarm said weakly. "I'll pay him."

"Good!" the doctor said, actually sticking out his fat hand.

"I mean, the government will when you submit a request."

"No! I want to be paid now!"

76

"Sorry," Longarm said, deciding he bore an intense dislike for this arrogant and insensitive man. "I'm a federal officer and you'll have to submit the paperwork to get paid. Same as I do with my expenses."

Carpenter let out a stream of cuss words that would have done any mule skinner proud. He stomped out of the room even before Longarm could dictate the address he'd need to write in Denver.

"What do I do?" Hank Walton asked.

"Take five dollars out of my wallet and give it to Dr. Carpenter," Longarm said. "That's plenty for the kind of service he rendered this morning."

"I agree," the cafe owner said with a tight smile. "With doctors like that, who needs to be shot in order to suffer?"

When the door closed again, Delia came over to stand beside Longarm. "Despite his boorishness, I'm still glad that you saw a doctor. I feel much better now, and we'll keep applying that salve until you are well again."

"Thanks," Longarm said. "As soon as I can manage it, I'm going out to have a word with Jesse."

"I don't think that's a wise thing to do."

"Maybe not, but someone tried to kill me and I've got to start finding answers before I become Agate's next murder victim."

Delia shook her head. "I've got some things to do downstairs. Will you be all right up here by yourself for a while?"

"Of course."

She left him alone then. Longarm's head was still pounding, and he closed his eyes, wishing for sleep.

It was evening when he awakened again, and his headache was completely gone. His room was dark except for a flickering kerosene lamp on his bedside table. There was no sound or movement in the room, but Longarm had the feeling he wasn't alone. He slowly sat up, and then noticed the silhouette of a man sitting in a chair not six feet from where he lay.

Longarm's first thought was that the dark and silent figure was the gunman intent on finishing what he'd started at the Ponderosa Cafe. Longarm sat up straight and frantically tried to see where his gun was resting so that he could grab it and defend himself.

"Relax," Jesse Jerome said, coming out of his chair and moving over to stand beside Longarm's bed. "I'm not the one that shot you last evening when you were having dinner with my woman. If I'd seen the two of you holding hands, I *would* have shot you. But I'd have come inside and braced you man-to-man."

Longarm stuck an arm out and turned up the lamp's wick so that it burned brighter. "What are you doing in here? Where is Delia?"

"I told her that I wanted to talk to you alone. I told her to wait downstairs. She didn't want to, which made me none too happy."

"Get this straight, Jesse. You don't own Delia and you never will."

The man didn't seem to hear him. "I was looking at you and remembering the second time that I saved your life. You had been wounded in the head—like now—and I sat beside your bed for two days wondering if you'd make it or if I was going to need a new deputy for my partner. You pulled through and you're doing it again."

"Why are you here?" Longarm demanded.

"I come to apologize for taking a swing at you out at the mine," Jesse replied. "And for not warning you to be extremely careful in Agate. There's a killer on the loose, and I'm sure whoever it is doesn't appreciate your investigation."

"I appreciate your concern, but how do I know for sure that *you* aren't that killer?"

"You don't," Jesse admitted. "But if you know me at all, you'll admit that I'm not the kind to leave a lot of

78

unfinished business. I take care of my problems directly."

"That's true of the old Jesse Jerome I once rode with, but I'm not sure it's true anymore. I've heard that you've got some hired gunmen on your payroll."

"That's a lie!" Jesse lowered his voice. "I have some guards that protect my valuable interests. That's only sensible. But I still handle my own personal problems."

Longarm was not sure that he believed the man, but said, "So who do you think shot me?"

"I haven't the slightest idea, but I've put out the word that I'll pay a hundred dollars reward for information."

"Generous of you," Longarm said, not impressed by the piddling figure.

"Yes, isn't it, though. But I didn't come to talk about the past. I came to talk about the future. My future. Your future . . . if you have one."

"Don't attempt to threaten me, Jesse."

"No threat," the rich man said. "I just want you to know that I take it very personally that you were taking liberties with my fiancée."

"Delia?"

"That's right. I told you before I intend to marry her and that I expected you to keep your business with her on a strictly professional basis."

Longarm heard the deadliness in Jesse's voice, and being in no position to anger him any further, said, "We had dinner together and I got shot by someone through the window. That's it."

"You had two bottles of wine and more to drink, and I heard she was on your arm!"

The big man was quivering with anger, so Longarm chose his next words very carefully. "Did you forget that I was raised in the South? I often escorted my mother to church on my arm. It didn't mean anything except that I had some chivalry and manners. Don't read more into it than it deserves."

"Look," Jesse said, pulling up a chair and scooting it

over close to the bedside. "I want you *out* of Agate! I don't trust you anymore."

"I'm sorry about that, but you know I was sent here to do a job and I can't leave until it's finished."

"Then I'll finish it for you."

"Meaning?"

"I think I know who the Scorpion Murderer is and I'm going to bring him to justice. Custis, leave Agate and don't ever come back. I promise you that I'll take care of things."

"Don't do it. If you know who killed the territorial governor and that reporter, then tell me his name and give me all you have as evidence and I'll do the rest."

"I have no evidence."

"Then tell me who you suspect."

"I . . . I can't."

"Why not!"

Jesse came to his feet. "I'll take care of this person in my own fashion. It may not conform with the law, but I'll guarantee you that he'll never harm anyone again."

"You know that's not good enough. What am I supposed to tell Billy Vail and the others when I get back to Denver? That you—the prime suspect—promised me you would 'take care of things' and mete out your own brand of frontier justice? Be realistic!"

"Is that your final word?"

"If you mean am I running out of town because you're threatening me, then yes, it is."

"I could kill you right now and get away with it," Jesse said.

Longarm swallowed hard because that was probably true. "What about Delia? She knows that you're up here in my room. Are you prepared to kill her too?"

"She's more reasonable than you are. I doubt that would be necessary."

"But what if it was?"

Jesse's hand came to rest on the pearl handle of his

revolver. "Custis, I'm sorry we were ever friends. I always held a special place for you in my heart."

"No, you didn't. You might feel some sort of friendship because we did go through some bad scrapes together. But you never had anyone in your heart except yourself. I well remember all the women whose hearts you broke with no more feeling than if you'd broken a beer glass."

"I'm leaving now. I'm going to take care of this Scorpion Murderer business, and when I do, I'm sure that the guilty party will also confess to shooting you in the cafe. As for Delia, if I so much as hear that you've been touching her again, you'd better be ready to defend your life!"

Longarm started to tell the man that he was thinking and acting crazy, but Jesse was out the door before he could form his words.

I'm probably going to have to either kill him . . . or be killed by him, Longarm thought. *He's laid down the challenge and given me no room to compromise. And I won't be intimidated or scared off, or that's the end of my pride as well as my profession.*

Suddenly, he heard a scream from down in the lobby. It was Delia, and there was no mistaking the sound of flesh striking flesh. Longarm jumped out of bed, found his gun, and took two steps toward the door before his head began to spin and he collapsed.

"Custis!"

He groaned and came back to the present. Looking up, he saw that Delia's eye was swelling shut and her hair was disheveled. "He struck you pretty hard, didn't he?"

"No."

Longarm blinked. "What do you mean, no?"

"It was someone else," Delia said quickly. "Let's not talk about it."

"Who!"

"Never mind."

"Delia, you can't keep me from arresting Jesse for as-

81

sault and battery. He did it. I know it and so do you. So just . . ."

But Delia shook her head and placed her forefinger hard to his lips. "Let's just forget what happened downstairs. There were no witnesses. You can't arrest someone without witnesses, and I won't say who hit me."

"You're trying to protect me."

Delia helped him back to his feet and then the bed. "Maybe I'm just trying to save *both* our lives."

Longarm understood, but his pride was injured. Jesse had struck Delia hard in the face and he needed to be thrown in jail. But Longarm also understood that he was in no shape to do that right now. So he swallowed his pride and allowed her to tuck the covers under his chin; then he watched as she went to his washbasin, poured water, and pressed a cool washcloth to her swollen eye.

"If I were able, I'd go after him right now," Longarm vowed, voice shaking with anger.

"He rode in with three gunfighters," Delia said.

She pulled the window shade slightly to one side and gazed down into the street. "They're all sitting on their horses in the street in front of my hotel . . . waiting to see if you're angry and stupid enough to rush downstairs and give them a chance to prove their marksmanship to Jesse."

Longarm ground his teeth together in frustration. He would just have to take this injustice and bear it in bitter silence. To do otherwise tonight would be suicide.

Chapter 9

Longarm must have fell asleep, because when he woke
up in the middle of the night, Delia Ballou was lying beside
him undressed and under the bedcovers. His lamp emitted
a soft yellow light that shone on her lovely face . . . the
face of an angel with a black eye. Just the sight of that
eye made Longarm's blood boil, and it was all he could
do to keep from jumping up, dressing, and going off to
find Jesse.

But the night was cool and Delia was sleeping peace-
fully despite her badly swollen eye. *If I were a man with
some money in the bank, I'd buy this hotel just so she
could get away from Jesse. But since I have no money,
I'll just have to take Jesse down a peg or two. He's gone
mad with his newfound wealth and sense of power. I
should have seen it in him before. Hell, I did see it in him
before when he hanged those men and shot so many others that he should have arrested and brought to trial.
Jesse Jerome hasn't changed. He's just gotten bigger,
bolder, and more dangerous.*

Longarm had to take a leak. He slipped out of bed,
steadied himself by holding on to the bedpost, then
headed for the door. His head stayed screwed on tight,

and he felt none of the dizziness that had dropped him to the floor earlier. He found the chamber pot and did his business, then climbed back into the bed knowing that he had turned the corner and would be fit and ready to go back to work soon, perhaps even in the morning.

"Custis?" she murmured sleepily.

"Go back to sleep," he whispered, smoothing her hair against the pillow and kissing her gently on the cheek.

"Are we going to get through this alive?"

"Of course. We'll be fine, Delia. But I was thinking that it might be a good idea for you to go away for a while."

She sat up. "No! I wouldn't leave you here."

"If Jesse knew we were lying in the same bed, he'd come storming in here and lead would fly," Longarm tried to explain. "It would be smart and make things far easier for us both if you left for a while."

Her injured eye was swollen completely shut, but she stared hard at him with the other. "Custis, I haven't run away yet. I'm not about to now."

"If you don't," he said, "it will trigger a gun battle between Jesse, his men, and myself. I've never seen him so jealous before. In fact, until you came into the picture, I never thought he was capable of that emotion. But now that I know he is, I think it would be far better for us both if you were temporarily out of the picture."

She hugged his neck. "Are you sure?"

"Definitely."

She took a deep breath. "All right. I'll ask Hank to take me to Prescott first thing tomorrow morning."

"That's not far enough," Longarm told her. "I want you somewhere that Jesse can't find you in a hurry."

"I suppose I could go to Flagstaff. I know people there I could stay with for as long as I wish."

"Then it's settled," he said. "Tomorrow morning, make arrangements to go to Flagstaff, only make it look like you went to somewhere else. Like Tucson."

"All right. But how on earth will I know how you're doing or when to return?"

Longarm frowned, then said, "I'll send you a telegram every few days just to let you know that I'm fine and when it is safe for you to return. How will that be?"

"I hate the idea of leaving you alone, but I do understand that jealousy could get you killed. Please be careful!"

"I haven't done much right so far, but I will from now on," he told her.

"Then why don't you start right now . . . with us."

Longarm felt her hand slip down his bare thigh. "Are you sure? You're an injured woman."

"And you're an injured man. We might hurt each other," she said with a smile. "But I'm willing to take that risk if you are."

"I am," he said, pulling her into his arms and feeling the heat of her skin against his own.

Longarm kissed her passionately, and she responded with a sudden and surprising ferocity. Then she grabbed his stiffening root and gently massaged its crown between her thumb and forefinger until it was standing tall and proud.

"Come on!" she urged. "I haven't had a man as big and strong as you since I was eighteen!"

Longarm was more than happy to do her bidding. He rolled her over onto her back and then climbed between her beautiful thighs. Lifting them up with his shoulders, he knelt poised for a moment, his rod teasing and probing her wet womanhood.

Delia moaned, and he poked the head of his manhood into her honey pot just a little ways, then moved it in and out as she continued to moan. "Curtis, you're going to torture me to death! Stop holding back from what we both want right now!"

He growled with pleasure and rammed his root deep inside her, feeling the heat and the wetness, and then he grasped her lovely hips and began to move them back and forth in union with his thrusting.

"Oh, my!" she groaned. "That's more like it! Don't stop!"

"Don't worry," he panted, thrusting and pulling harder. "I hope you're feeling as good as I am!"

In answer, she pulled him down tight on top of her and then stuck her tongue in his ear. She rolled him over and mounted him, then threw back her head and raised herself just enough so that Longarm could enjoy her lovely breasts. Delicious moments passed as they rocked back and forth and Longarm laved her taut nipples.

"Can we keep doing this all night?" she breathed, eyes shut tight and lips pulled back from her teeth.

"We can try," he replied, losing himself in the feeling.

When Delia finally rolled off, he pulled her up to her hands and knees, then mounted her from behind like a stallion, slamming her hips against his own until her head dropped and she begged for satisfaction.

Longarm took her hard and deep. He thrust until she shouted with pleasure and her buttocks began to twitch; then he sent his hot seed far up into her womanhood, reveling in his own glorious passion.

She collapsed and he sagged down upon her, his rod still pumping the last drops of his seed with slow, dogged determination until he was drained dry.

"Delia," he said, rolling her over onto her back. "That was one of the best. . . ."

Her lips silenced his compliment and she kissed him gently. "Just love me as much as you can tonight and let's not talk. I've heard nothing but words for so long now, and what I need tonight is your body and my body doing what they were meant to do since the moment we were both born."

Longarm collected her in his arms, thinking that this could be one of the most unforgettable nights of his entire life. There was something about this dark, mysterious beauty that fired his passion like few women he'd ever known.

I'm going to count the days until she returns from Flagstaff, he thought. *It's going to be hard, but I won't let her come back until it is absolutely safe for her to do so.*

Delia fell asleep in his arms. He dozed off as well, and it was dawn when she found his manhood with her mouth and he awakened with his pulse pounding.

"Beautiful woman," he said, watching her pleasure him. "Where have you been all my life?"

A few moments later he was riding her again and, if anything, with even more passion than during the night before. He took longer, and used their bodies until they were gasping, straining, and begging for relief. Then, he brought them to a dizzying height, and when Delia cried out with pleasure, he found his own moment of shining, shuddering ecstasy.

Chapter 10

Longarm had watched Delia leave Agate in a buckboard headed south and driven by Hank Walton, who had closed up his cafe for a few days. Longarm wasn't the only one that watched the pair leaving, and he knew that their departure and direction would soon be relayed to Jesse Jerome.

All I have to do is wait here and he'll be along in an hour or two, Longarm told himself. *The real question is, how many gunmen will Jesse have when he gallops into town?*

Longarm went back up to his room and lay down for a few minutes because his head was aching again. He must have slept for a while because he awakened to hear someone hammering on his door.

"Custis!" a familiar voice bellowed. "Unlock the door or I'll bust it down!"

"Hold on."

Longarm drew his pistol and stepped up to the door. "Come on in, Jesse. But you'd better not have a gun in your hand."

"Where'd she go?" Jesse asked the moment he was inside.

"To Tucson."

"What for!"

"Delia needed some time away from here," Longarm told the angry mine owner. "She thought it might be healthier for everyone if she left Agate for a while."

"I'll find her," Jesse vowed, starting to leave.

Longarm decided to take matters into his own hands. He knew Jesse wouldn't cooperate with him, so he took a step forward and brought the barrel of his heavy Colt revolver down hard against the side of the older man's skull, striking him just behind the ear exactly as Jesse had taught him to do years earlier.

Jesse collapsed and Longarm locked the door. He moved over to the window and glanced down into the street. There were three mounted gunmen. Longarm shouted at the trio, "Your boss said it was okay for you boys to go get a drink at the saloon."

They all started with surprise and craned their heads back to stare up at Longarm. One of them yelled, "We'd like to hear that from Mr. Jerome!"

"He's taking a siesta."

"Huh?"

"A nap," Longarm explained. "Jesse was tired and fell asleep."

The three gunmen began to discuss this. Longarm closed the window knowing that, if they had any sense at all, they'd go have a few drinks and decide that maybe it wasn't such a good idea to interrupt their boss's nap.

Longarm had a pair of handcuffs in his traveling bag, and after he applied them to his old friend, he stretched out on his bed and waited for Jesse to regain consciousness. It didn't take long.

"Damn you, Custis! I'll get even with you," Jesse moaned.

Longarm sat up. "I'm considering arresting you for attempting to murder me in the Ponderosa Cafe."

Jesse's eyes burned. "That wasn't me that fired at you."

"Then who was it?"

"I don't know, but I sure wish he'd been a better shot."

"All the evidence points to you in the Scorpion Murders, and you're also the only one jealous enough to try and kill me just for holding hands with Mrs. Ballou."

"I didn't try to kill you!" Jesse shouted. "But if you're more interested in protecting yourself than getting things right about those murders, then go ahead and arrest me even though you haven't a single shred of real evidence."

Longarm knew this was closer to the truth than he cared to admit. "If you didn't kill Governor Stanton or that newspaper reporter by turning scorpions loose on them . . . who did?"

"I'll take care of who did it by myself." Jesse sat down on the bed and studied his manacled hands. "I put a lot of these sonsabitches on prisoners, but I never expected to be wearing a pair of them myself."

"Life is full of bad surprises," Longarm told the man. "Who is the Scorpion Murderer?"

"It's . . . Buster."

"You mean that dull-witted gate guard?"

"Has to be him."

Longarm was suspicious. "I don't think Buster has the intelligence to commit murder. Besides, what would have been his motive?"

"He's . . . he's my kid brother," Jesse said with unmistakable bitterness.

Longarm found a chair. "I don't believe that."

"It's true. I never told you about Buster because he was always . . . well, simpleminded. I was ashamed of him. When I won the Agate Mine, I learned that Buster was locked up in an institution down in Phoenix. He'd hurt some men real bad, nearly killing them with a busted beer bottle."

"He must have inherited your temper."

"He did," Jesse admitted. "Buster was teased constantly as a child. I did some of it myself, but he always looked up to me as his idol. I was bigger, stronger, far smarter, and better-looking. I got the women and Buster just got teased. So he'd fight. I disowned my brother many years ago."

"So why didn't he stay disowned?"

Jesse looked away. "The idea of me being rich and Buster being locked in an institution preyed on my mind, and finally, I bought his freedom. After that, I brought him up here and gave him a simple job guarding the mine gate."

"Even if I believe that story, it doesn't explain why he would kill the former governor."

"That swine Stanton insulted me. He was saying things that were untrue, and he made the mistake one night of talking me down in front of Buster."

"If that was the case, I would have expected your simpleminded brother to have hauled off and shot or beat him to death. Not waited until Stanton was asleep, then cover him with deadly scorpions."

"That's because you don't know Buster." Jesse wiped more blood from his scalp. "You see, he is dumb, but being locked in an institution made him cunning. Buster is just smart enough to know that, if he wants to hurt or kill someone again, he has to do it so he won't be caught."

"But with scorpions?"

"Buster has always been fascinated by poisonous critters and snakes. He has a way with them actually. I'd once told him how I'd thrown scorpions at big Diamond Jim Brady. Buster laughed when he heard that story, and talked about it for months. He said that was a good way to scare or kill a man who'd tried to hurt you in word . . . or deed."

"So that's why you said you'd take care of it yourself?"

"Buster is my brother, but I can't let him kill everyone that insults me."

"Jesse, do you have any proof that Buster is the Scorpion Murderer?"

"Only that I found a dead scorpion or two in his little cabin up in the hills the last time I was there. They were the same especially poisonous variety that killed the governor and the reporter."

"Did you ask Buster about them?"

"Yes, but he clammed up and ran off. He was scared, and wouldn't even face me for days. When I brought up the subject again, he got angry. But it has to be Buster. He's the only one that had any reason for killing Stanton and the reporter."

Longarm got up and began to pace back and forth. "Do you know what could happen to Buster if he is judged guilty in a court of law?"

"He'll be sent to an asylum for the criminally insane. And frankly, that would be the best thing for Buster. Otherwise, he's probably going to kill again and again."

"The last time we met you told me how rich you were and how valuable your time was. Would you be willing to help me track your brother down and deliver him to the authorities?"

"I would."

"Do I have your solemn word that you won't turn on me?"

"What's the matter?" Jesse asked. "Don't you trust me?"

"No, I don't."

"Custis, I'm calling in old debts. I saved your life twice. Now you got to at least give me a chance to save my brother from killing anyone else and then getting caught and lynched."

Longarm could see no way around it except to honor the man's wish. He wasn't going to buy into the story until they found Buster, and then he'd know for sure . . . one way or the other.

"Okay," he said. "But if you give me even the slightest reason to think you're going to do something to cause me

93

death or harm, I'll put a bullet in you faster than a buck rabbit can screw a doe."

Jesse managed a grin. "That's pretty damn fast."

"And so am I," Longarm said, the memory of his night with Delia crossing his mind. He wouldn't ever mention that to Jesse. And if it became an issue later, well, he'd cross that bridge when it needed crossing.

Longarm unlocked the handcuffs. "Do you have any idea where your brother might have gone?"

"There's an old fur trapper's cabin hidden up in the high mountains, and Buster likes to go there when he's feeling pressured or sad. It's just about ten miles north of Flagstaff."

It was all that Longarm could do not to groan. That was where Delia had gone. Tarnation! It seemed his run of bad luck was never going to change.

Chapter 11

Longarm didn't want to go to Flagstaff and maybe run into Delia, but as he rented the sorrel and prepared to leave town, he figured that there was no choice. The afternoon was growing late when Longarm rode up to the Agate Mine. Buster had been replaced by a new gate guard, and the man waved him on toward the mining shack.

As soon as Longarm reined his sorrel gelding to a stop, Jesse stepped outside flanked by several of his gunmen. For a moment, Longarm was sure that his old friend was going to force a showdown, but Jesse said, "My saddle horse and a pack animal are being readied out back. We can leave in a few minutes. I see that you didn't bring either a bedroll or food."

"I remembered that you liked to travel in style, and I figured you'd take care of everything we need."

"I have," Jesse said. "My cook even packed us a couple of steaks for tonight along with some sliced and seasoned potatoes and a bottle of wine."

"That's great," Longarm said without much enthusiasm. "How far is the old fur trapper's cabin?"

"It's about seventy miles and nearly all uphill. I'd say

that two days of hard riding ought to get us there," Jesse answered. He turned to one of his men and said, "Get a bedroll for the marshal and throw it on the packhorse."

"Yes, sir!"

One of the gunman said, "Boss. Are you sure we shouldn't come along? What if . . ."

"I'll be all right," Jesse told the man. "You just make sure that no one steals me blind while I'm gone."

"I'll watch out for your interests."

"See that you do," Jesse said.

His horse, a big palomino, was brought around saddled and ready to ride. The packhorse was a stout bay gelding. Jesse took the reins and mounted. "Just like old times, huh?"

"Not exactly," Longarm replied. "Let's go."

They galloped across the wagon yard and out through the gate. Longarm let Jesse lead the way, figuring the man probably knew the shortest route to Flagstaff.

They'd ridden hard all through the late afternoon, and made camp among the pines. Longarm gathered wood for their fire and Jesse unpacked their supplies. He had always liked to cook and was good at it, so Longarm let the man take care of preparing supper. By the time the steaks and potatoes were ready and the wine was poured, the sun had disappeared behind the mountains and the air was taking on a chill.

"Here," Jesse said, handing Longarm his meal. "If I recall correctly, you like your meat a little more raw than I do. Kind of bloody on the inside."

"That's right," Longarm said, taking his plate and nodding with approval when he cut into the steak. "Good job."

"You like it, huh?"

"I never had such a fine meal out on the trail," Longarm answered. "We never ate this way in the old days."

"That's because we were both poor." Jesse took a bite

of his steak, added a little salt, and nodded with satisfaction. "When you have money, everything goes better."

"I'm sure that's generally true."

They ate in silence, watching the night deepen. Finally, Jesse said, "I want you to promise me something, Custis."

"What's that?"

"When we find Buster, let me handle him. Just stay back so that he doesn't panic and do something stupid."

"Like what?"

"I don't know. Maybe try to kill you."

"Or you?"

Jesse shook his head. "He'd never try to kill me. I'm his idol, remember?"

"Yeah."

"So what do you think of Delia?"

Longarm continued to cut his steak. He forked a piece into his mouth and chewed it thoughtfully before asking, "What do you mean?"

"I mean, are you interested in her?"

"She's nice and I enjoyed her company. But you remember how it was when we worked together on a field case. You meet women. Some you remember, most you forget."

"Delia isn't the kind of woman any man would forget."

"That's true." Longarm took a sip of wine. "She's afraid of you, Jesse. She doesn't want you bothering her anymore."

"That's what they all say to begin with. She'll change her mind soon enough."

"Don't count on it."

Jesse tossed down his wine and poured another glass. "I remember how, when we used to travel, you were always the strong, silent type. I had a good line with the women, but you never had to say much to get them interested."

"That was quite a while ago."

"Yeah, but I have a feeling that not all that much has changed."

Longarm said nothing.

"Delia isn't quite the lady you think she is," Jesse added. "She's got her dark side, like the rest of us."

Wanting to change the subject, Longarm asked, "Do you think we can find Mike Kelly up in Flagstaff? I'd like to have him tell me to my face how you won his gold and silver mine."

"Even if we did run across Kelly, he wouldn't tell you anything. He's too proud to admit that he lost a fortune that night. He'd probably say that I cheated him."

"Did you?"

"I told you that I got lucky enough to beat him despite his dealing from the bottom of the deck." Jesse stared across their campfire. "Seems to me that you're looking for any excuse you can find to brand me a liar and a murderer."

"You know that isn't true," Longarm countered. "You did save my life, you know, and I'd like nothing better than to prove you innocent. It's just that—so far—you're the only one with the means and the motive."

"You know what I think?" Jesse asked. "I think that you resent my getting lucky and rich. That's why you're so determined that I'm the Scorpion Murderer, despite the fact that everything you know about me ought to tell you that isn't my style. I'm innocent, and my only regret is that Buster is our killer."

"Why don't we wait until we find him and then hear his confession." Longarm's eyes narrowed. "Your brother *will* confess, won't he?"

"He will if I tell him to."

The way that Jesse said that made Longarm wonder if Buster could be coerced into a confession for something he did not do. "Look," Longarm told his old friend. "We've got a long ride tomorrow, so why don't we just finish up these steaks, then bed down and get some sleep. Daybreak will come early."

"Suits me fine," Jesse said. "I was just trying to make friendly conversation."

Longarm ate the rest of his supper in silence. He finished his glass of wine, then checked to make sure that their horses were securely tied to the picket line before he returned to his bedroll and stretched out preparing for sleep.

"You're going to trust me not to get up in the night and kill you in your sleep?" Jesse asked, sounding amused.

"I am."

"Hmmm. I'll bet that you sleep with your gun in your hand. You always were a light sleeper out on the trail. I imagine that hasn't changed much."

"That's right."

"Don't worry," Jesse told him. "I'm going to behave. I want Buster to be arrested and taken to an insane asylum where I know that he'll at least be fed and cared for no matter what happens to me."

"Are you expecting to die, Jesse?"

"One never knows when his time is up. And like I said, I feel guilty for the way I treated Buster when we were kids. There was a time early on when he was happy and harmless. I'd be a liar not to admit that I had something to do with changing him into a murderer."

Longarm didn't know what to say about that, so he pulled up his blankets and gazed at the stars. Jesse had always been quick to fall asleep, and he wasn't one to wake early. Longarm figured that hadn't changed either, and so he waited until he heard the man begin to snore before he also fell asleep.

They arrived in Flagstaff late the next day, feeling sore and tired from their long hard ride. Longarm was hoping that they wouldn't accidentally run into Delia, and given that the town was large and bustling, he thought that chance meeting somewhat unlikely. After boarding their horses and checking into a hotel, they decided on an early supper.

"Where is this cabin where we can find Buster?" Longarm asked after eating and leaving the cafe.

"It's only a couple of hours north of town," Jesse answered. "Look, why don't we go over to that saloon and have a couple of drinks? Maybe we can find a game and make some money."

"You know I'm not much of a gambler."

"Well, I'd sure enjoy a game. And since I'm not formally charged with murder, I take it that I'm free to come and go as I please."

"Not exactly."

"Let's go have a few drinks," Jesse urged. "It's too early to turn in yet. Come on! I'm buying."

Longarm had no choice but to agree. He followed the ex-lawman into a saloon called the Birdcage.

"Well, I'll be damned!" Jesse whispered. "Custis, this must be your lucky day."

"Why is that?"

"See that big fella sitting at the poker table with his back to us?"

"The one with the red hair and silk shirt?"

"That's the one and only Mike Kelly."

Longarm started to move forward, but Jesse grabbed his arm and hauled him over to a corner where they could speak without being overheard. "Why don't you let me handle this my way?" Jesse asked.

"And how would that be?"

"I'll just mosey on over as friendly as anything and sit down at that empty chair and tell those boys to deal me in. Mike won't like it, but he can't stop me from playing. Then we'll see what happens when I start to tell the others at the table about how I skinned him out of the Agate Mine."

Longarm didn't understand. "What's that going to prove?"

"You'll see when he explodes. Mike has a temper as bad as my own. He'll probably accuse me of cheating and I'll have to kill him."

"Oh, no, you don't."

"Hell, Custis, the man is a cheat. If you watch carefully, he'll deal from the bottom of the deck when the betting is heaviest."

"I didn't come here to catch a card cheat," Longarm said. "I just want to have him tell me that you won that mine in a game."

"Then let me give him some bait," Jesse said. "He'll bite and it'll be plenty clear enough that I beat him out of a fortune that night in Agate."

Longarm considered this for a moment, and decided that Jesse had a good point. If Mike Kelly reacted violently to taunting, that would probably mean that he had been bested at his own game.

"Okay, but be careful. If he's as hotheaded as you are, he might go for his gun."

"I expect that's true," Jesse said a moment before walking toward the poker table, "but I also expect that you will be right behind him with your own gun in your hand."

Longarm watched closely as Jesse sat down at the game, and there was no mistaking Mike Kelly's instant and angry reaction.

"Jesse, you're not welcome here!" Kelly shouted.

"Oh, now come on, Mike. We used to play cards all the time together. No cause to be unfriendly."

"I'm warning you to get out of my sight!"

There were three other men at the table besides Kelly, and they all got up and hurried away, leaving the two big men to glare at each other. Longarm moved in closer, his eyes on Kelly's gun hand.

Jesse was in a taunting mood. "I'm sure sorry that you

101

still feel so bad about losing that mine. You know, it turned out to be worth a lot more than either of us could possibly have imagined."

"Yeah, I heard about that."

"Too bad you lost it."

"I'll live," Kelly hissed. "But you may not."

"Ah," Jesse said, his face splitting into a wide smile. "Now there's no need for you to be making threats. All I want to do is play a few hands of cards for old times' sake."

"Get out of my sight."

But Jesse ignored the warning and took a chair at the table. "What are we playing tonight? Five-card draw?"

"I ain't playin' nothing with you," Mike snarled. He started to get up from the table and leave, but Jesse grabbed him by the wrist and cried, "What's that I feel under your coat sleeve? Could it be a spring-loaded card feeder?"

Before Mike could form a protest, Jesse yanked up the gambler's sleeve to reveal the device, and then he yelled, "Hey, look, everyone! How about this!"

Kelly yanked his arm free, then made a grab for the gun on his hip, but Jesse hammered him in the face with a brutal overhand right that sent the gambler to the floor.

Longarm kicked the man's gun away and shouted, "Kelly, you're under arrest."

"Who the hell are you?" the gambler demanded to know as he shook his head clear of cobwebs.

"United States Deputy Marshal Custis Long. Get up and keep your hands out where I can see them."

Kelly did as he was ordered. Longarm frisked the man and found a derringer in his vest pocket and a knife in his boot top. Satisfied he had all the gambler's weapons, he gave Kelly a hard shove toward the saloon door saying, "You're going to jail."

"For what!"

"Cheating at cards and the attempted murder of Jesse Jerome."

Kelly swore under his breath, and Longarm gazed around the room for a moment before he prodded the gambler outside with the barrel of his gun, then got him started for the town jail.

There was just one deputy on duty, but he seemed intelligent and efficient. He locked Kelly up, and told Longarm that the gambler would be facing a circuit judge the following week.

"Just watch out for him," Longarm warned.

"You'll need to fill out a statement," the deputy said, pushing a pad of paper in Longarm's direction. "And you'll need to be here when Kelly is brought before the judge."

"I'll try," Longarm replied.

He sat down and wrote out a hasty statement detailing how Mike Kelly had gone for his gun after a card-dealing device had been exposed under his sleeve. When he finished the brief report, Longarm headed back for the Birdcage Saloon.

"Where did he go!" Longarm shouted at the bartender.

"Who?"

"Jesse Jerome!"

"He left right after you," the man said. "I just thought he was tagging along after you to the jail."

Longarm hurried back outside. Jesse was nowhere in sight. *I got no one to blame but myself,* he thought. *I should never have trusted him.*

But a half hour later, he found Jesse sitting in on a high-stakes poker game at one of the other saloons.

"Hey, Custis!" the man shouted as Longarm stomped over to glare down at his old friend. "My luck is running strong tonight. I've already won sixty dollars."

"You're through for the night," Longarm told Jesse. "Cash in your chips."

103

"Hey," a mule skinner argued. "He's got to give us a chance to win back our money!"

"Sorry," Longarm told the man.

"Well, sorry sure as hell don't cut it with me," the mule skinner bellowed, coming to his feet.

Longarm pulled back the lapel of his coat to show his federal officer's badge. "Mister, if you don't sit down and close your mouth, you're going to jail."

The mule skinner sat down and stared at his pile of chips. He was mad, but sober enough to know when to keep quiet.

"Let's go," Longarm told his old friend.

"Well, boys," Jesse said, "I'm sorry that I took your money, but I'm going to buy you all a bottle of whiskey. I want no hard feelings being held against me for having a little luck."

Jesse did buy the table a bottle of the saloon's best whiskey, and this gesture won him the friendship of those whose money he'd just won.

"You always need to leave them smiling whenever you can," Jesse said as he and Longarm headed back to their hotel. "That's something I always remember to do."

"Well, you must have forgot when it came to Mike Kelly."

Jesse snorted. "Kelly is a cheat and a sore loser. I don't give a damn what he thinks of me. And anyway, I'm sure that you could tell by his reaction that I won his gold mine."

"Yeah, I could tell," Longarm replied.

"So tomorrow morning we go and find my brother. But you have to remember that I'm the one that does all the talking. Otherwise, he could get panicky and do something dumb."

"You mean like going for his gun?"

"That's right," Jesse said. "And I don't want that to happen."

"You can have first crack at getting him to surrender,"

Longarm agreed. "But if you fail, then I'll have to make the arrest."

"Fair enough," Jesse said. "I just don't want any harm to come to Buster."

Longarm nodded with understanding. He didn't want any harm to come to Buster either. In the first place, he needed to talk to the man and make sure that he actually was the Scorpion Murderer. And in the second place, it would be wrong to gun down a simpleton.

Chapter 12

Longarm was up early the next morning, and he made sure that Jesse was too. They dressed, ate a big breakfast, and went to the livery to get their horses.

"The cabin where I expect to find Buster isn't that far," Jesse said as they prepared to ride out of Flagstaff. "We ought to be there in two hours and back by noon."

"That sounds good to me," Longarm replied, tightening his cinch. "Let's ride."

They headed north up toward the San Francisco Peaks, following a logging road through the heavy stands of pines. The air was cool and there wasn't a cloud in the pale blue sky. A soft breeze rippled through the pines, and towering Mt. Humphries was still mantled with fresh snow. All in all, Longarm thought, it would have been a fine day just to ride off toward the Grand Canyon and make a day of sightseeing. Unfortunately, that wasn't going to be the case. They were after Buster, and Longarm couldn't shake the feeling that something was going to go wrong.

"That's the trail to the cabin," Jesse said, pointing. "I'd guess it's about five more miles."

"Lead off," Longarm said, preferring to keep the man in front rather than behind. "I'll follow."

"What's the matter? Do you think I'd shoot you in the back?"

"You know the trail and I don't," Longarm replied, avoiding a direct answer to the man's question.

They rode single file along a narrow, winding game trail. To his right Longarm could look down into a deep gulch thick with trees and manzanita. To his left was a ten-foot wall of granite rock and then more trees clinging to the side of the craggy mountain. A blue jay screeched at them from above as they followed the trail ever higher until they rounded a bend and saw an old log cabin about a half mile off in the distance. The cabin was half hidden by trees, and could easily have been missed except that smoke trickled from a stovepipe that protruded from a rough shingled roof.

"Looks like Buster is here," Jesse said.

"Where is his horse?"

"There is a small corral just behind the cabin."

Longarm took in the scene. "I'll circle around behind the cabin so he can't jump on his horse and escape. You ride up to the door and call him out. Tell him that he'll have to go back to Flagstaff and answer some questions. Make sure he's unarmed."

"All right," Jesse agreed. "Just don't shoot him."

"You know I wouldn't cut down a man without reason."

They separated, and Longarm sent his sorrel into the trees moving at a trot. It took him nearly fifteen minutes to get around behind the cabin, and by then, Jesse was riding across the meadow in plain view.

"Buster!" he shouted. "It's me, Jesse! Come on out. We have to talk."

Longarm dismounted, tied his horse to a pine, and moved around the cabin. Jesse was sitting on his horse

108

about thirty feet in front of the cabin, waiting for Buster to appear.

"Come on!" Jesse urged. "There's nothing to be afraid of. I won't hurt you!"

They waited a few more minutes, and then Jesse dismounted and led his horse right up to the cabin door, which was hanging open. Longarm stayed hidden until he heard Jesse cry, "Oh, no!"

Longarm hurried around to the front door of the cabin and peered inside. Jesse was kneeling over a body, and Longarm was pretty sure that it was Buster.

"Is he dead?" Longarm asked after a few moments.

"Yeah," Jesse choked.

He dragged Buster out of the cabin by his ankles. Buster was shoeless and shirtless. There was a bullet hole that entered under his right ear and exited the opposite his skull just above the left ear.

"Let me look around in there," Longarm said, moving into the cabin. "Maybe I can find some clue as to who killed your brother."

Longarm searched every stinking inch of the cabin, but he found nothing to indicate who the killer might be. By the time he emerged, Jesse was already at work digging a grave for Buster. There were tears in Jesse's eyes that Longarm knew could not be faked.

"Did you find any evidence of who murdered my brother?" Jesse choked out.

"I'm afraid not. Do you have any suspects in mind?"

Jesse shook his head. "I can't imagine who would do such a thing."

"I wonder if it had anything to do with the Scorpion Murders," Longarm mused aloud.

"Hell, no! They happened too far from here."

"Someone might have been in on it beside your brother and wanted to shut him up permanently."

Jesse had a shovel in his fists, and for just the briefest instant, Longarm thought the man might try to use it to brain him. But Jesse regained control and sighed. "I can't think of anyone that would have wanted Buster dead."

"Someone did."

"Maybe it was just a common thief that took something from my brother and then killed him for no real reason."

"Maybe," Longarm said, doubting that theory. "But did your brother have anything worth stealing?"

"He had a good Colt revolver that I bought for him, as well as a bone-handled pocketknife. Both are missing. Other than those two things, he didn't own anything of value."

"I'm still inclined think that his death might have had something to do with the Scorpion Murders."

Jesse drove the shovel deep into the soft meadow and hurled a shovelful of dirt away. "I have no idea who killed Buster or why he was shot. It looks to me like he's been dead only a few hours."

"Then maybe we can find some tracks," Longarm suggested.

"I'm going to bury him before I do anything else."

Longarm nodded with understanding, and then he walked all around the cabin until he discovered a set of horse tracks. They were fresh, and so he went back to the corral and took a good look at the hooves of Buster's horse. The tracks were from a different animal.

"Looks like I found our killer's trail," he said a few minutes later, pointing southeast back in the general direction of Flagstaff. "Let's finish up here and get moving."

They laid Buster deep in the dark, damp earth and covered him with dirt and sod so that his grave was unmarked and would go unnoticed.

"Let's ride," Longarm said impatiently.

Jesse climbed into the saddle. "Where are those tracks you found?"

Longarm showed him, and then they pushed their horses into a gallop, following the tracks across the mountain meadow and back into the forest. Whoever had left the cabin had been in a hurry. You could tell that by the way the tracks were cupped by a horse running fast through the forest.

"Slow down, Jesse, or you'll get us both killed!" Longarm shouted as they raced through the trees at breakneck speed.

But Jesse wasn't listening. He was bent over his saddle horn and riding like a wild man. Longarm had little choice but to just try and keep up with his old friend as they wound their way through the heavy vegetation and finally burst out of the trees and back on the same logging road that had brought them out of Flagstaff.

"Dammit!" Jesse shouted, leaning far out of his saddle and studying the tracks. "There's too much traffic on this road to make out the one we want to follow!"

The man was right. The logging road was well traveled and there were dozens of horse tracks, some from big wagon horses and others from those under saddle. Longarm dismounted and studied the churned-up road, hoping that he was wrong.

"We're out of luck," he finally decided aloud, glancing up at his friend. "There's no way we can make out the tracks we were following."

Jesse swore bitterly and slammed his clenched fist down on his saddle horn. "Whoever did it is in Flagstaff," he said. "Maybe someone will remember seeing a lone rider galloping into town."

"We'll sure ask people we meet if they saw anyone," Longarm said. "But that won't mean they saw the one that killed Buster."

"Maybe not, but it's all we have to work with."

Jesse spurred his horse into a gallop, heading down the road toward town. Longarm's sorrel wasn't the palomino's equal, and he let Jesse ride on ahead.

• • •

111

"Did you see anyone at all come riding in from the north," Longarm asked each and every rider and wagon driver that he met coming up the mountain road.

"No, sir," they all told him, until he reached the outskirts of Flagstaff and saw an old woman tending her flowers.

"Ma'am, did you happen to see a lone rider come riding into town from the north an hour or two ago? He'd have been coming fast and his horse would have been heavily lathered from hard running."

The old woman pushed her sunbonnet back and stared up at Custis. "Who is asking me?"

Longarm showed her his badge. "Ma'am, it's very important."

"I did see a rider come galloping by about two hours ago. It was still early and I was pulling weeds from my carrot patch when she went racing past on a sweaty horse. I remember—"

"Whoa!" Longarm interrupted. "Did you say *she*?"

"I'm pretty darned sure it was a woman . . . but I can't be positive. She was dressed like a man but she had long, dark hair hanging down the back of her shirt. Her hat was pulled low over her eyes, but I could see that she was young and brown-skinned. It could have been a young Mexican or Indian. Whoever it was kept whipping that horse. Kinda made me angry the way she was beating after the poor, worn-out beast."

"Delia," Longarm whispered, then added, "But you're not sure it was a woman, are you?"

"No, I ain't. But it wasn't a full-sized man either. Like I said, it could have been a boy, but if it was, he had long, shiny hair."

"Do you remember what the rider's horse looked like?"

"It was a bay with a long black tail and mane. Had a white stocking or two, I think."

"A star or blaze on its face?"

The old woman closed her eyes for a moment, then

pursed her lips. Finally, she said, "It had a white blaze on its face. I remember that clearly now. It was a smallish animal and so winded it was puffing like a steam engine. Poor thing was about ready to give out."

"You've been very helpful," Longarm told the woman. "I sure do appreciate your help."

"Who is Delia?"

"Just a person."

"Did she do something wrong?" the woman persisted. "Or is she running from someone? Marshal, it ain't fair to ask me curious questions, then ride off leaving me wondering what this is all about!"

"I'm sorry, ma'am. But I need to find the rider of that horse and ask her some questions."

"Shouldn't be too hard to find that little bay horse. Unless he's been washed and brushed real good, he'll be caked with lather and sweat. You ought to find him easy enough."

"Thanks, ma'am."

Longarm rode away, deciding not to tell Jesse about this because neither of them were prepared to think that Delia Ballou might have something to do with Buster's death, much less killing the man herself. If Longarm found the little bay horse, he would probably be able to learn the identity of its rider. And when he did that, they'd have the answer as to who murdered Buster Jerome, and he sure hoped it wasn't Delia.

Chapter 13

"I'm going to get stinking drunk tonight," Jesse announced that evening as they prepared to go out for something to eat. "And tomorrow, I'm going to tear this town apart until I find out who killed my brother and the reason why."

Longarm frowned. "Both of those are bad ideas. I can't stop you from getting drunk, but I sure can keep you from raising hell."

"Look," Jesse said as he pulled on his coat and reached for his hat. "We've been friends a long, long time, and I don't want us to have a showdown."

"Neither do I," Longarm said. "But I know how wild and ornery you get when you've had too much to drink and you're in a bad mood. I've seen it many times, and I can't let you get into trouble."

Jesse glared at him. "Someone murdered my brother! Do you expect me to take that lying down?"

"No. I expect you to behave and then go back to Agate tomorrow. I'll stay here to do the investigation."

"Not a chance."

Longarm stepped up to his friend and said, "Jesse, I still don't have a clue as to who is behind the Scorpion

115

Murders. You say it was your brother. If that's true, then someone must have followed him up to that cabin and killed him in revenge."

"I thought of that, but it doesn't wash because Buster had no real enemies. The reporter that died had no friends out here in the West, and Governor Stanton was roundly disliked by everyone outside of his own family. And on top of that, no one but me knows Buster was the Scorpion Murderer."

Longarm placed his hand on Jesse's broad shoulder. "We don't have to cross swords, Jesse. But you do need to behave yourself and leave Flagstaff in the morning."

"Are you *ordering* me back to Agate?"

"Yes."

Jesse turned and walked to the door. He paused, then looked back at Longarm before saying, "All right. But you have to promise me that you'll find out who killed my brother."

"I'll do my best. You know that, Jesse."

"Yeah, I guess I do." He managed a thin smile. "Let's get something to eat and then get drunk together just like old times."

"I'm not going to do that," Longarm decided out loud. "One of us has to stay sober and keep the other out of trouble."

"All right then. You're the sober one and I'll be the drunk one."

"And you'll leave Flagstaff first thing tomorrow morning?"

"I'll have a hangover. Might not be able to go until afternoon."

"That's close enough," Longarm said. "But if you get too rambunctious and troublesome, I'll give you another crack across that thick skull of yours with my pistol."

"You can try," Jesse replied, his voice taking on an edge.

• • •

They had supper and went saloon-hopping. At each establishment, Jesse would order the best whiskey in the house, and then he'd demand that he be dealt into a poker game for a few hands. Longarm drank beer, and was content to stay back out of the way as long as Jesse behaved himself. But as the evening wore on and Jesse began to get drunk, the man became more and more belligerent and abrasive. He was having good luck with the cards and accumulating a considerable amount of money, but he was a poor winner.

"You dumb bastards don't know how to play poker!" Jesse swore as he raked in a pile of crumpled greenbacks. "Why, I'm almost ashamed of taking your money!"

One of the players, a slender, well-dressed man, made the mistake of replying, "If you're feeling so sorry for us, why don't you get lost. No one asked you to join this game."

Longarm saw Jesse stiffen, and he knew that the former lawman was about to do or say something that would provoke the smaller man into a fight.

"Jesse," he said, hurrying over to the table, "it's time we called it a night."

But Jesse wasn't listening. "Mister," he said to the man who had dared to suggest he leave, "I don't appreciate being told to get lost."

"That's just too damn bad."

Jesse started to reach across the table and grab the man by the throat, but Longarm's hand shot out and locked on his wrist. "Jesse, collect your chips. You're done playing tonight."

Jesse threw his arm aside, trying to break Longarm's grip. When that didn't happen, he lurched to his feet and used his left hand to try to strike Longarm in the face. But Custis easily ducked the punch, and he shoved Jesse backward into another table. Before Jesse could reach for his side arm, Longarm grabbed a glass of beer and tossed it into his face, temporarily blinding him.

117

When Jesse was able to wipe his eyes clear, he was staring down the barrel of Longarm's pistol.

"Collect your winnings and say good night to the gentlemen whose money you won," Longarm ordered.

Jesse shook with fury, but collected his money and said, "Good night, gentlemen. This is Deputy Marshal Custis Long and when he draws his weapon, he never bluffs. Do you, Custis?"

"You know that I don't. Let's go."

Jesse turned, threw back his shoulders, and slowly made his way to the bar. "Bartender, I want a clean towel."

"Yes, sir!"

Jesse mopped the beer from his face, then from his neck and collar. He studiously ignored Longarm until he was dry, then reached into his coat pocket and brought out a handful of dollars. Placing them on the bar top, he said, "Drinks on the house. Your best!"

"Yes, sir!"

Jesse turned and grinned at the men whose money he'd just used to buy the drinks. It wasn't a friendly grin, but instead a triumphant sneer. Then he pulled his hat brim lower over his eyes and headed outside with Longarm right behind.

"Dammit!" Custis swore. "Why'd you have to act like that!"

"Because they were a bunch of fools," Jesse replied with contempt. "Compared to me, they were just pretenders. Why, I could have cleaned them out if you'd let me play longer."

"Let's go back to our room," Longarm said, barely able to curb his own anger. He gave Jesse a hard shove toward their hotel. "And the first thing tomorrow morning, you're heading for Agate."

"Don't push me, Custis!" Jesse shouted, whirling around and raising his big fists.

"Put your hands down and let's get some sleep."

"I'm not done with my drinking."

"I say you are."

Jesse drew a derringer from somewhere and cocked back its hammer. "What do you say about *this*?"

Longarm felt a shiver go up his spine. Jesse was drunk and he was mean. More than that, he was plenty capable of killing anyone in anger. "Jesse, just put the gun away and let's call it a night."

"I don't think I want to do that," Jesse said, the derringer surprisingly steady in his fist. "And I have had about all of you that I can stand."

Longarm's mouth went dry with fear. He inwardly cursed himself for not pistol-whipping his old friend again and then carrying him back to the hotel. That mistake might just cost him his life in the next second or two. "Jesse, don't—"

Suddenly, a gunshot split the night air, and Jesse doubled up with a groan and staggered back against the front of the saloon.

Longarm drew his own gun and searched in vain for the shooter. Not seeing anyone, he grabbed his old friend and dragged him back toward the saloon door. Just as he was pushing Jesse inside, a second shot caught the ex-deputy in the back, causing him to throw up his hands and fall face-first to the saloon floor.

Longarm whirled, gun still clenched in his fist. He couldn't see anyone across the street, but was sure that was where the shots had originated. Either on the ground or up on the roof.

"Custis!" Jesse wheezed. "Help me!"

Longarm dragged Jesse farther into the saloon. "Bartender, bring me some towels and find a doctor!"

Longarm knelt beside his friend. Jesse was in bad shape. The first bullet had caught him in the groin and it might or might not prove fatal. The wound was bleeding heavily, and Longarm unbuckled Jesse's pants, then shoved a towel over the bullet hole. He rolled Jesse over,

119

and saw that the second bullet had stuck him below the right shoulder blade. He could hear Jesse laboring hard for breath, and figured it might have pierced his lungs.

"Dammit, get a doctor!" Longarm shouted as the bartender and most of the saloon patrons gathered around in a circle to stare in morbid fascination.

"I'll get Doc Hoskins!" the bartender said, tearing off his apron and barging outside.

Longarm heard the man's boots pounding down the boardwalk. He pulled Jesse's shirt up and pressed a bar towel over the wound. Then he gently rolled Jesse onto his back and stared down at the man's pale face.

"I bought it, didn't I?" Jesse wheezed. "I'm finished."

"I don't know. Just keep still and quiet. A doctor is on the way."

"I don't think he can do anything," Jesse whispered. "Someone has gone and killed me. Killed me just like they killed Buster!"

"Don't quit on yourself," Longarm pleaded. "You're still a big, strong man. You can make it through this if you save your strength and we can get the bleeding stopped."

Jesse managed a smile. He tried to laugh, but a bloody froth formed on his lips. "I'm lung-shot and we both know that I'm dying. It might take a while, but I'm finished."

"I don't know that," Longarm said harshly.

"Find out who killed me and Buster."

"I will. I promise."

"Don't arrest 'em . . . kill 'em!"

"Just be still. I've seen lung-shot men pull through. You've got two lungs and you can make it on just one."

"Custis, you never were any damn good at lying."

After what seemed like forever, but was probably less than five minutes, a portly man with a bald head and wire-rimmed glasses slammed through the doorway.

The bartender was right behind him, face flushed with excitement, and he gasped, "This is Dr. Hoskins."

"Stand aside," Hoskins ordered, opening his medical kit and kneeling next to Jesse. "Where is he hit?"

Longarm told the doctor, who then rolled Jesse over and quickly examined, then re-bandaged the wound. Next he checked the wound in Jesse's groin and said, "This man is losing far too much blood. We have to get him over to my operating room table and try to stop the hemorrhaging."

Longarm agreed. There was no way that they could hope to save his old lawman friend while he was lying on this barroom floor.

"We need a flat surface to carry him on," Hoskins said, looking around. "Break the legs off one of those poker tables and use it as a litter."

This was done immediately, and then they eased Jesse onto the poker table and five men grabbed its edges and carried him back outside. As they struggled to carry the big man down the boardwalk to the doctor's office, Longarm couldn't help but wonder if the shooter who'd brought Jesse down was still hiding and watching in the dark shadows across the street.

Dr. Hoskins had them lay Jesse out on a heavy wooden table stained darkly with blood. Longarm shoved everyone else out the door, and went over to his wounded and perhaps dying friend. "How are you holding up?"

"It's a good thing that I'm drunk, or this would really hurt," Jesse managed to joke.

"Are you his friend?" Hoskins asked.

"Yes," Longarm replied.

"Then I'll tell you both right now that your friend's chances are poor."

"Hell, we both know that already, Doc!" said Jesse.

"Shut up and save your strength," Hoskins ordered. He turned to Longarm and said, "Hold your friend steady while I try to dig the first bullet out of his groin."

"Aren't you even going to give him something for the pain?"

"He's already too well medicated with liquor," Hoskins snapped. "Now do as I say!"

Longarm nodded in agreement. He watched Hoskins pull Jesse's bloody pants down to his knees, followed by his underwear.

"They didn't shoot off my big snake, did they, Doc?" Jesse asked, trying to smile.

"Shut up and don't move!" the doctor snapped.

Longarm watched as Hoskins selected a long-nosed forceps from a metal pan filled with foul-smelling disinfectant. A moment later, Jesse's back arched and he screamed as the forceps probed deep into his flesh.

"Hold him still!" Hoskins bellowed, blood pouring out of the wound as he probed even deeper. "If we don't get this bullet out, he hasn't a chance."

Longarm needed every bit of his weight and strength to hold Jesse down on the table, until the man suddenly let out a cry and his body went limp.

"Doc, is he dead?"

Hoskins grabbed Jesse's wrist and found a pulse. "Not quite," he said as he went back to his bloody work of attempting to dig out the lead slug.

It was past midnight, and there was nothing more that Longarm could do for his old friend. The doctor had managed to dig most of the lead out of Jesse's groin. And as for the other slug in his back, there was nothing that could be done. Further probing would kill him for sure.

"It's out of my hands and in God's now," Hoskins told Longarm at the door. "Most men with wounds like that would have died already. Your friend is exceptionally tough."

"He always was," Longarm replied. "What are his chances?"

"They're poor to none," Hoskins answered without hesitation. "I can't say for sure that he'll die. Miracles do happen. But it would take a miracle for him to pull

122

through with those wounds. And he's lost way too much blood."

"Yeah."

"Any idea who shot him?" the doctor asked.

"No," Longarm said. "Whoever it was was hiding in the dark just waiting to ambush Jesse."

"Or you?"

Longarm blinked. "What do you mean?"

"You're a federal law officer, aren't you?"

"Yes, but . . ."

"And you were both wearing dark clothes and are about the same size."

"I don't think I was the intended victim."

"I merely bring up the possibility in case there is someone out there who wants you dead. If that is the case, you'd be wise to use every precaution to avoid a second ambush."

"You're right," Longarm said with reluctant agreement. "I could have been the target, but he didn't make any friends tonight as we made the rounds of saloons. He insulted a lot of men."

"Who is he?"

"Jesse Jerome owns the Agate Mine and half of the town of Agate. He's rich," Longarm said in the way of explanation. "But he used to be a regular working federal marshal like myself."

"Some men lose control when they get money. They destroy themselves. I've seen it happen more than a few times."

Longarm didn't know what to say about that, so he just nodded and started to leave.

"Marshal, watch your back."

"I will."

"Who pays my fee when he dies?"

"I'll pay you," Longarm said. "But you said he might pull through."

"I said that miracles happen, and it would take one for

your friend to survive those two bullet wounds. As strong as he is, the man could linger on for days. Marshal, go back to your room, lock your door, and get some sleep."

"Will you stay with him?"

"I'll be right here in this old chair at his side," Hoskins promised, pointing to a stuffed chair in the corner of the operating room. "If Jesse calls out, I'll be here."

"All right then," Longarm said on his way out the door.

He went back to the street, then searched for some evidence that would at least tell him where the assassin had hidden and fired at Jesse, or himself. But it was too dark to do anything of value, so Longarm returned to the hotel, went up to his room, and promptly fell into a restless and troubled sleep.

Chapter 14

Longarm slept until ten o'clock the next morning, then awoke with a start and quickly dressed. He didn't take the time to shave, but just splashed some cool water in his face before grabbing his hat and hurrying out the door. He reached Dr. Hoskins's office in a few minutes, and when he barged inside, he was shocked to see Delia Ballou standing beside Jesse with tears in her eyes.

"Delia, what are you—"

"The news of the shooting is all over town. I heard about it this morning and came here at once." She reached out, took Jesse's hand, and squeezed it hard, tears filling her eyes. "I am completely devastated!"

Longarm damned near dropped his teeth, but Jesse made a gurgling sound in his lungs, capturing his instant attention. His old friend looked terrible. Jesse's skin was waxen and his eyes feverish, but he was staring up at Delia as if she was an angel to be adored. "Delia, you won't leave me, will you, darling?"

"No," she passionately vowed. "I'll *never* leave you again."

It was all Longarm could do to keep his silence. Obviously, there was something going on between these two that had been very well hidden. Delia and Jesse must have been lovers at one time either before or after the death of her husband.

Longarm felt betrayed and deceived, and perhaps it showed on his face because Delia gave him a wan smile. "Custis, I know this comes as a surprise. And I know that I said some things that don't make sense right now, but—"

"You sure as hell did!"

"Whatever I said before doesn't matter now because Jesse is going to make it!" Delia told him in a voice filled with determination. "He's going to pull through this and we're going to get married."

"What?"

Jesse roused to stare at Longarm. "This is the only woman I've ever really loved. I want you to be my best man."

Longarm couldn't believe what he was hearing. "Jesse, we can talk about this when you get stronger."

"No," his old friend said, breaking into a coughing fit that brought up a bright, bloody froth. When he finally got control, Jesse glared at Longarm and wheezed, "I intend to marry Delia *now*."

"You're talking crazy!"

"Yes," Dr. Hoskins said, pushing into the room. "That's what I told Mr. Jerome."

"Delia, get a preacher," Jesse gasped, eyes rolling in his head. "If Custis won't stand in as a witness, find someone on the street and pay 'em. Hurry along, now!"

Longarm reached out and grabbed the woman, but she flung his hand aside. "Marshal, this isn't about you. It's about Jesse and me!"

When she left, Longarm leaned over his friend, who was again struggling for breath. "Jesse, are you in your right mind?"

"I am," he snarled. "I love Delia. I didn't tell you this before, but I'm sure that Buster poisoned her husband because he knew I loved Delia and desperately wanted her as my wife. Now, I'm going to marry her and, if I don't make it, I want her to inherit *everything* I own."

"But I don't think she even likes you!"

Jesse's eyes burned, and his voice was a tortured hiss as he whispered, "She *does* love me!"

"But . . ."

"I'm going to make it," Jesse rattled. "Delia is with me, and now I really have something to live for. But even if I should die . . . she's the only person other than yourself who matters."

Longarm sat down in the chair, removed his hat, and ran his fingers through his long hair. Jesse closed his eyes and struggled for every breath.

This is insane! Longarm thought. *What is going on here?*

"Marshal?"

He glanced up to see the doctor motioning him out of the room. He followed the man into a cluttered office, where Dr. Hoskins took a chair behind a battered desk.

"Marshal, that man is your friend, so I have to tell you that he will not live to enjoy consummating his marriage."

"Are you positive?"

"Quite. He's bleeding internally. Slowly drowning. He'll be dead by noon."

Longarm shook his head. Jesse was hard, even cruel, but he was an old friend, they'd been through some tough times together, and the man had saved his life. Suddenly, Longarm realized that he would miss Jesse Jerome despite all his many glaring faults.

"What I want to know," Hoskins said, "is if this marriage can be stopped."

"I don't see how," Longarm replied. "I'm no lawyer, but Jesse is still alive and able to make his own decisions."

"What about relatives?"

"Jesse has no family. He had a brother, but the man was just murdered."

"Are you going to allow this marriage to take place?"

"I can't see how I have any authority to stop it," Longarm said. "I mean, the man wants to marry Delia."

"Tell him he is about to die," Hoskins ordered. "Tell him there are charities and good causes that his money could be used for. I don't—"

"Doc," Longarm interrupted. "Jesse's mind is made up, and I'd just be wasting my breath. He doesn't care about charities. He loves Delia Ballou and thinks that she can help him pull through."

"But I'm telling you as a doctor that he will die very soon!"

"And I'm telling you that we can't change Jesse's mind."

Hoskins removed his wire-rimmed glasses and rubbed the crown of his nose. He replaced the glasses and said, "Marshal, are you aware that when that man dies without a will or heir, his estate goes to the Territory of Arizona to be used for good public works?"

"I'm from Denver and haven't given the matter any thought."

"Isn't that better than it all going to someone who might even have had a hand in his death?"

Longarm stiffened. "Doctor, what exactly are you saying?"

"Think! Mr. Jerome is ambushed last night by an unknown assassin, and now this woman shows up to inherit his fortune. Doesn't that seem a bit odd or even suspicious?"

"Yes," Longarm said, surprised that the possibility of Delia having anything to do with the shooting had not yet occurred to him. It would have before long, but this morning things were so crazy that all he'd been able to think of was of Jesse's death or survival.

"So, Marshal, what are you going to do about that young woman?"

"There's nothing I can do without some proof. If Delia brings back a preacher in the next few minutes, I'm going to honor my friend by agreeing to be his best man and witness to the marriage."

Hoskins snorted with disgust. "You're being a fool. If that woman is behind your friend's death as I suspect, you'll never forgive yourself for allowing this marriage."

"If she's behind it," Longarm said, "I guarantee she'll never get the chance to profit from Jesse's death."

Hoskins started to say something else, but was interrupted when the door to his office banged open. He peered around the corner and said with obvious distaste, "It's the Reverend Gideon Carter."

Longarm stood on one side of the Reverend and Delia on the other as the vows were quickly exchanged. "I now pronounce you man and wife," Carter solemnly intoned.

Delia cried, and Jesse tried to keep from coughing up blood. The bride must have told the minister the circumstances were unusual, because the man carried a marriage certificate, and it was immediately signed by the couple and witnessed by Custis.

Jesse's skin had a bluish tone and his eyes were dull with pain, but he managed to smile and say, "Thanks, Reverend. Custis. Now you two can leave us lovebirds alone."

Longarm ushered the Reverend outside and when he demanded his fee, Longarm gave him ten dollars. Carter hurried off looking annoyed and disappointed.

"Well, you did it," the doctor said as he came outside to sit beside Longarm on the wooden porch.

"Doc, I'll tell you for the last time. I had no choice. If I'd refused to stand in as a witness, Jesse would have sent for a stranger. It was the least I could do for the my dying friend."

"No," Hoskins said, "the least you can do for him is to

129

find out who killed him. And I'm betting that, if the woman herself didn't fire the shot, then she paid someone who did."

"You're a cynic."

"I'm a realist," Hoskins countered. "And if you weren't all emotionally confused and wrapped up in this mess, you'd realize that what I'm telling you is the only thing that makes any sense."

"I knew that Jesse loved her." Longarm shook his head. "I just didn't know that Delia secretly loved him. That's the part that *really* threw me."

"Marshal, maybe you're not as intelligent as I'd first thought," Hoskins said a moment before he stood up and walked back into his office.

Longarm got some breakfast. He then went back to the Birdcage Saloon and walked through the shooting, and then returned to where the shooter might have been hiding. He didn't find anything. Not a footprint, a matchstick, or a single clue.

Was Doc Hoskins right about Delia being behind the shooting? Had Buster Jerome been the one who'd murdered not only the former governor but also the reporter and Delia's husband?

Longarm had never felt so overwhelmed by uncertainty. Every step he took in this investigation turned a surprising corner that led him into a dead end.

What the hell am I going to do? Go back to Denver and tell Billy Vail and the others that a half-wit named Buster Jerome was the Scorpion Murderer? That he also killed a man named Homer Ballou because he thought, in his simpleminded way, that so doing would make Delia available to his lovesick brother? And what if that was exactly the way it had all happened? But how could I be sure?

Dr. Hoskins was wrong. Jesse didn't die at noon, but instead lived almost until the following morning. Then, with

130

Delia weeping at his side, the rich man from Agate passed on over the Great Divide.

Longarm wasn't at Jesse's side when he finally gave up his heroic struggle and breathed his last. But when he arrived at the doctor's office for the second morning in a row, Delia was waiting for him with her red and puffy eyes.

"I want to take his body back to Agate," she said. "He told me that he'd like to be buried there in the little cemetery. I want Jesse close so that I can see his grave from my bedroom window."

"You mean from your window in the Agate Hotel?"

"No, of course not. I'll be moving into our mansion."

"Just like that, huh?"

She gave him a strange look. "Jesse wanted me to live in his mansion. He wanted me to have all the things that I've never had before and that he could give me either in life . . . or in his courageous death."

"I see."

Delia took his arm. "I know you're confused about this."

"That's an understatement. You told me in bed that you hated him, and I had no reason to doubt your words."

"I . . . I wasn't being completely honest."

"Obviously not."

"Don't be cross with me," Delia said, fresh tears filling her eyes. "We've both been through so much these last few days. You loved Jesse in your way and I loved him in my way. Can't we let it go at that?"

Longarm didn't think he could, but thought it smarter not to say so. Instead, he nodded and said, "Let's get Jesse's body to that cemetery in Agate. I don't want to talk about anything else for a while."

"Nor do I." Delia sniffled. "Let's rent a hearse and be gone. Hank can drive it."

Longarm was surprised. "You mean the fella who owns that cafe in Agate?"

"Yes. Hank Walton who brought me here. Don't you remember that?"

"Sure, but I thought he would have gone back to Agate."

"He intended to, but decided to stay a few days. He's such a good friend."

"Yeah, I guess he is," Longarm said, his mind spinning. "Where is Hank now?"

"He'll be along soon," Delia told him as she took his arm and they started walking.

"Where are we going?"

"To the livery to rent a hearse, of course. Then to get something to eat. I haven't eaten since I heard that poor Jesse was shot. I'm feeling quite weak."

"I'm sure you are," he said, wondering about Hank Walton.

Chapter 15

Hank drove the hearse back to Agate while Longarm rode the sorrel and led Jesse's fine palomino along behind. There wasn't much to say on the return trip. Longarm watched Delia and Hank closely, trying to see if he could detect something deeper than respect and friendship. But he saw nothing out of the ordinary.

News of Jesse's death had somehow preceded them to Agate, and by the time that their hearse rolled down the main street, the townspeople were in a state of high excitement. They were grinning, cheering, and dancing in the street. It was then that Longarm realized how much his old friend had been hated and envied.

Funeral arrangements were made that same morning, and the service and burial were at noon in a stark little cemetery. The town's only minister was the same man that Longarm had met on the stage ride to Agate. His eulogy was anything but complimentary, and he ended it by saying, "Jesse Jerome was a hard, dangerous man who took *what* he wanted . . ."

Staring hard at Delia. ". . . *when* he wanted and *how* he wanted. He won't be missed, but he will be remembered. I don't know if he was a soldier of Satan, but now that he is gone, perhaps we can remake Agate into the God-fearing town that it once was."

Longarm glanced over at Delia to see if she was upset by those hard words, but the woman seemed not to be listening. Her eyes were fixed on the casket and the grave that it was being lowered into.

Another familiar face at the funeral was the woman Longarm remembered meeting on the stage over from Prescott and whose name was Carol. She and her husband stood back a ways and said nothing, nor did they show any emotion. Funny thing was, *nobody* seemed upset, not even Jesse's employees. There wasn't a single tear shed among the crowd of some eighty or ninety observers. And for some reason, that made Longarm even more depressed.

"Rest in peace and may God have mercy on your no-good soul. Amen," Reverend Crawford said before he turned around and raised his hands to the crowd. "Ladies and gentlemen, this marks the end of darkness and the beginning of hope and light for Agate. Now, I invite you one and all to come to my church and celebrate our blessings!"

Longarm was surprised to see that at least half the crowd did follow the Reverend Crawford down to his little chapel at the south end of town.

"That was the worst eulogy that I've ever heard," Longarm told Delia and Hank. "I should have stepped in and said a few words in defense of Jesse. The man did some good things in his life. He wasn't all bad."

"No," Delia agreed, pulling aside her black veil. "Jesse had some fine qualities. Compassion just did not happen to be one of them."

"He did all right by you, Delia," Longarm heard himself say in a voice that carried an accusation. "You're a rich woman now."

"Yes. Jesse loved me. And because of that, I have a chance to right all of his wrongs."

Her words caught him off guard and he blurted out, "What does that mean?"

Delia looked down at Agate from the vantage point of the cemetery. "It means that I'm going to restore prosperity to this town. I'm going to sell off the businesses for only a few cents on the dollar and I'm going to bring new hope and investment to Agate."

"Delia has it all planned out," Hank Walton said, looking at her with pride. "She wants to make this a good town again . . . one where working people can live in peace and prosperity."

"Really?" Longarm said, unable to hide his suspicions.

"That's right," Hank said. "We're going to turn things around here in a big hurry."

"What about the Agate Mine?" Longarm asked.

"I'm keeping that," Delia said without a moment's hesitation. "You don't give away the golden goose."

"I see." He looked at Hank. "And are you planning to expand your cafe and business interests?"

"I hope to," the man told him. "I mean, if Agate starts to boom again, why wouldn't I?"

"Can't think of any reason," Longarm answered.

"I suppose that you'll be going back to Denver now that we know that Buster Jerome was the Scorpion Murderer."

"No," Longarm said, "not just yet. I still need to know who killed Buster and Jesse."

Hank clucked his tongue sympathetically. "That's going to be real hard to figure. Did you question Mike Kelly when you were in Flagstaff?"

"Only to confirm that he did lose the mine to Jesse in a poker game."

"If you ask me," Hank said, "Mike Kelly is your killer. You need to go back to Flagstaff and find him before he disappears. I'll bet that, if you squeeze him hard enough, he'll confess to killing both Buster and Jesse."

The rancher's wife, Carol, was standing nearby, and

135

when she heard this comment, she reacted with surprising anger. "Mike Kelly didn't kill Jesse or that half-wit Buster. He's a gambler, not a gunman."

"Oh, hi, Mrs. Dunn," Hank said, then turned to the tall, rugged-looking cattle rancher. "How you doin', Link?"

The tall, rugged-looking rancher nodded. "I'll get by."

Carol Dunn said, "Marshal, forgive me for speaking out of turn, but Mike Kelly befriended my husband once, and he became a friend to both of us. We found him to be an honest, decent man."

"That's *your* opinions," Delia said sharply. "I also knew Mike Kelly, and I'll guarantee you that he was no saint."

"And neither are you," Carol snapped. "How can you be such a flaming hypocrite to have married Jesse Jerome on his deathbed! And now you want everyone in town to think of you as their savior. Well, I think you're a Jezebel and a fraud, Mrs. Ballou!"

Longarm jumped between the two women a moment before Delia would have attacked Carol Dunn. "Easy, ladies. Jesse Jerome is dead and has just been buried. Why don't we let him rest in peace?"

"He's not resting in peace," Carol spat a moment before leaving. "Jesse's burning in hell!"

Longarm had to restrain Delia until Carol Dunn was well out of reach. "Easy," he said, finally releasing her. "The woman is just upset."

"She's more than upset," Delia said. "She and her husband tried and tried to get Jesse in trouble. They're the ones that spread the most vicious rumors about him being behind the Scorpion Murders."

"Why would they do that?"

"Because Jesse dammed up their main source of water for his mining operation. Beaver Creek runs through my mining property and we need that water, but when Jesse tried to explain that to the Dunns, they reacted as if he'd cut their throats."

"If Beaver Creek was their main source of water for

their cattle, then maybe Jesse did sort of cut their throats."

"They have another creek they can use," Delia said. "But it's going to have to be diverted and channeled a few miles to be accessible to their range. They didn't want to spend the money, so they began to attack Jesse, accusing him of every crime and bad thing to happen around Agate."

Longarm nodded, only beginning to see how deep and widespread the animosities ran in this part of the country. Not that he was surprised at how many people had hated Jesse. That was evident by the celebration their arrival had touched off when the people had seen Jesse stretched out in a hearse. But what did surprise him was how complicated the divisions were. He'd never heard anything about Beaver Creek, and suspected there were many other issues that lay hidden mostly from public view.

I'm really going to have to start digging in order to find the killer or killers of Jesse and Buster, he thought. *And maybe I ought to make it a point to talk to Carol Dunn and her husband.*

Longarm spent the rest of the afternoon in Agate talking to people about Jesse. Most of what he heard confirmed that Jesse had been ruthless both in his personal and his business dealings. A man suggested that Longarm talk to a young horse trader named Annie Martin who owned a homestead a few miles south of town.

"She knew Jesse as well as most anyone," he said. "I think she genuinely liked the man, and she would stand up for him when she heard someone putting him down in public."

"Were they . . . sweethearts?" Longarm asked, preferring to use that word rather than lovers.

"Naw. If anything, Annie treated Jesse like a father. Or maybe a big brother."

Longarm took the suggestion to heart and rode out to see Annie. He met the young woman as she was arriving from a shopping trip from Prescott. Annie was only about five feet tall, with brown hair and large brown eyes. She had rosebud lips, a big bosom, narrow hips, and a no-nonsense way of talking. She wasn't beautiful like Delia, or even as attractive as Carol Dunn, but she had a wholesomeness about her that bespoke of spending a lot of time out in the sunshine working with her horses. Annie wore a boy-sized pair of pants, a workingman's red flannel shirt, chaps, and spurs. With a battered Stetson pulled down low on her brow, she could have easily been mistaken for a small cowboy, except for the size of her chest.

"You have a nice little place out here," Longarm told her, looking at the corrals, barns, breaking pens, and finally the log cabin. "I can see that you put a lot of work into keeping it in good repair."

"I try."

Longarm couldn't help but notice that her brown eyes held flecks of gold, and there was a swath of freckles over her nose and upper cheeks. She was even more attractive than he'd first thought.

"How many horses are you breaking right now?"

"Six," she told him. "I buy and sell them mostly in Prescott. Sometimes I'll take on an outlaw if he has the stuff to make a good saddle horse. Some of them, though, are just bad to the bone and can't be saved. They don't start out as outlaws, but someone sometime has messed them up so bad they can't be saved."

"I see."

"Do you like horses?"

"I do."

"That old sorrel you rode in on is one that I sold to Jesse about four years ago. Would you believe that he was once a bad bucker and biter?"

"Nope," Longarm said. "He seems pretty tame to me now."

"He's a good old pony," Annie said, striding over to the sorrel to scratch him behind both ears. She hugged his

138

head and stroked his muzzle for several moments. "This horse was always one of my favorites. I'm glad to see that you didn't run him out here. He deserves to be ridden easy, and that way he'll stay sound for quite a few more years."

"I won't use him too hard," Longarm promised. "Did you also sell that palomino that Jesse rode?"

"Yes, I did," Annie said. "Where is that horse now?"

"He's still at the livery in Agate."

"Delia thinks she can ride him, does she?"

"I don't know."

"Tell her to stay away from that horse because he's too strong for her to handle. I try to match the horses I sell to the people who buy 'em. I won't sell a spirited animal to a poor or even average rider. People get hurt on horses that are too much for them."

"I'm sure that's right."

"Who are you?" Annie asked.

"My name is Custis Long. I'm a United States deputy marshal from Denver."

"Custis Long," she repeated. Her face lit up in a wide grin. "Well, I'll be damned! Jesse used to talk about the days when he wore a badge and you rode together! Never thought I'd meet you, though. He didn't tell me you were so big and handsome."

Longarm had to chuckle. "Jesse was quite a few years older, but we hit it off right away."

"I'm sorry that he was killed," Annie said, her boyish smile dying. "Jesse could be meaner than a teased snake and twice as dangerous, but he was the kind of man that always told you where you stood. I admire that in people. There was never any doubt about the way he felt about you . . . one way or the other."

"I understand that you were close friends."

"We were," Annie said. "Say, why don't you help me unhitch the wagon after we unload the grain sacks and supplies? Have you had anything to eat lately?"

"Not since breakfast."

"Then stick around and I'll rustle us up something good. We can talk about Jesse, if you like."

"I would like," Longarm said. "Do you live out here alone?"

"That's right. I had a husband once, but he got kicked in the head by a big paint horse and then he got mean. He used to try and whip me, and sometimes he did. Jesse caught him doing it once and damned near beat Jethro to death. After that, Jethro threatened to kill us both. Next thing I know, Jethro is gone and he ain't never come back. I don't want him back now. I did for a long time, because it's hard for a woman who is used to having a man suddenly having her saddle empty. Know what I mean, Marshal?"

"Custis," he said. "Uh . . . yeah, I guess I do."

"Aren't you married?"

"Nope."

"That's surprising, given how big and handsome you are. Do you like Arizona?"

"Sure."

"In that case," she said, giving him a wink, "maybe you ought to stick around awhile after supper and we can get better acquainted."

Longarm had to smile. This was one of the most direct women he'd ever met, even if she did smell like the horses she so loved.

Chapter 16

Longarm helped Annie unload a ton of oats in hundred-pound sacks. He was amazed at how she could lift and carry them as easily as most men. After unhitching her buckboard and caring for her horses, they carried some food into the cabin and Annie prepared a simple supper of beans, bacon, and fried potatoes, washed down with water from a good-tasting spring she had out behind the cabin.

"Do you smoke?" Annie asked when supper was finished and the cleaning up was done.

He patted his coat pocket. "I enjoy a cigar."

"I like to smoke my father's corncob pipes," she told him. "Let's go down by the corral and watch the horses until it gets dark. We can talk about Jesse."

"You already knew that he was dead," Longarm told her as they walked out to be near the horses.

Her face clouded. "I knew it right away. There's a young Indian fella named Tall Tom who comes by now and then. I give him something to eat in exchange for him helping out around the place. He told me just this morning about Jesse getting shot to death up in Flagstaff. But I knew Jesse was going to get hisself killed one of these days. We talked about that some a time or two."

"You did?"

"Yep. Jesse said that someone was bound to show enough gumption some day to do him dirty. He told me that he didn't want a funeral ceremony or any words to be spoken over his grave."

"I'm afraid that he didn't get his wish on that score," Longarm told her, remembering the funeral service. "The Reverend Crawford didn't have one nice thing to say at his eulogy."

"Crawford is a self-righteous soul," Annie said, not bothering to hide her distaste. "I wouldn't trust that man as far as I could throw him. He's big on pointing out the faults of others, but you'd never hear him admit making a mistake. He's a hypocrite. Jesse wasn't, though. He admitted his many faults, then went right on with his life."

"The reason that I came out here to talk is that I don't have any idea who killed him," Longarm admitted. "I've been a law officer for a number of years, and I have to confess that this case has me baffled. I don't even have a real suspect."

"A lot of people hated Jesse enough to do him in."

"So I've learned."

"How'd it happen?" Annie asked. "Jesse was pretty good with a gun and he was wary."

"He got careless and drunk," Longarm explained. "We were coming out of a saloon and someone ambushed us from across the street. It was dark and I didn't even have time to see the muzzle flashes."

"I hope Jesse didn't die too hard," Annie said quietly.

Longarm changed the subject. "Delia was at his side and they got married."

"She married Jesse Jerome on his deathbed?"

"That's right. She's now the owner of the Agate Mine, his mansion, and half of the town of Agate."

"Well, knock me over and kick me in the head!"

"Does that news upset you?"

"Why should it? Jesse loved Delia in the worst way. I think she was the only thing he ever loved, but she wouldn't have much to do with him. As far as I know, she was faithful to her late husband."

"Then I take it you like Delia?"

"I don't know her all that well, but from what Jesse told me about her, Delia is a straight shooter. We all have our dirty laundry, but as far as I know, she was on the up and up. I am surprised that she married Jesse. I'll bet most of the people in Agate are green as grass with envy."

"Actually," Longarm said, "they're not. Delia has promised to sell back the town buildings and businesses that Jesse gobbled up for a pittance. She swears that she's going to bring prosperity back to Agate again."

"I'm glad to hear that. Bet she hangs onto the mansion and the mine, though."

"You're right about that."

Longarm watched Annie fill a corncob pipe, tamp it thoughtfully with a forefinger, then strike a wooden match on her belt and light it. He stuck a stogie in his mouth and they smoked together in an easy silence for a while.

"Were you wondering if Delia had Jesse shot so she could marry him and inherit his wealth?" Annie finally asked.

"As a matter of fact I was."

"And that's what you really came out to ask me? What I think of her?"

"And a fella named Hank Walton."

Annie leaned her forearms across the top rail of the corral and watched the horses for a few moments. "You know, I learned from my father that you can't read a horse by his looks. There are bad horses that look gentle and gentle horses that will pin their ears back every time you step close but they wouldn't hurt you for anything in the world."

"I'm sure that's so."

"It is," Annie said, making a soft gurgling sound as she

143

sucked on her pipe. "And it's the same with some, but not all, people. Now I knew that Jesse Jerome was a son-ofabitch the first time I saw him. I didn't have to ask anybody. But, in his own way, he was an honest sonofabitch. He wasn't sneaky."

"Is Hank Walton sneaky?"

"I think he is," Annie said. "I mean, he never said nothing bad to me or about me. He always smiles and is pleasant enough, but Jesse sure didn't trust him. He told me that Hank loved Delia almost as much as he did."

"So you're saying that Hank might have ambushed Jesse that night up in Flagstaff?"

"He might have. I can't say. I just know that he carried a lot of hatred toward Jesse . . . but then so did most folks."

"Annie, you're talking in circles."

"I've told you that I don't think Delia had anything to do with Jesse being killed even though she is the one that wound up with all his money. I told you that Hank might have been behind it. It wouldn't surprise me if he tries to marry Delia as quick as he can. But I think he loves her so much that he'd marry Delia even if she was still broke."

Longarm smoked on that for a few minutes. "I've been told that Mike Kelly, the gambler, might be behind the killings."

"Killings? You mean there were more than one?"

"I guess you didn't know that Jesse's brother Buster was murdered that same day. Jesse and I rode up to Flagstaff to find him shot to death in some mountain cabin."

"Well, I'll be damned and diddled! Buster was murdered?"

"That's right. Jesse told me that his brother was the Scorpion Murderer."

"Well, I'll be doubled damned and diddled!"

"Do you think that's true?"

"Yes," Annie said. "Buster was not only addle-brained,

he was vicious and crazy. I wasn't going to say it, but he was at the top of my list of suspects."

"All right," Longarm mused, "so let's assume that Buster *did* kill that reporter and Governor Stanton. I'll probably never be able to prove it, but I'm beginning to think that he was the one. However, that still leaves me trying to figure out who killed Jesse and Buster."

"I'd watch Hank Walton and Link Dunn."

"The cattle rancher who was feuding with Jesse over the water coming down Beaver Creek?"

"That's right. Link is a dangerous and difficult man. He shot and killed two fellas who were stupid enough to try and rustle a couple of his yearlings. And after he shot them up, he hung 'em from a big old pine tree just to warn anyone else they better stay off his ranch."

"He hanged dead men?"

"Yep. And no one dared to ride onto the Dunn Ranch and cut them down. Finally, Jesse and a couple of his men went over there and did it. They buried what the buzzards had left of the cattle rustlers. Link and Jesse had words over that too. I told Jesse many times that Link was maybe the only man in this part of the country that wasn't afraid of him. Link doesn't say much but he is dangerous. His wife, Carol, is mouthy but nice, and so are their kids. But Link is deadly."

"Maybe I should pay a visit to his ranch."

"You better have a reason, or he'll just tell you to get off his place and do it quick."

"He can tell me whatever he wants," Longarm said, bristling. "But I'm working on an official murder case and he'd better tell me what I need to know or I'll haul him into town and toss him in jail."

Annie shook her head. "Link wouldn't take to being arrested. He'd go for his gun."

"I appreciate the warning. Did you know Mike Kelly?"

"Only that he's a gambler and that he lost the Agate

145

mine to Jesse. I have no idea if he could have killed Buster and Jesse."

Longarm shook his head. "I feel like a branch being blown back and forth in the wind."

"I'm glad that all I have to do is to break and train horses," Annie told him. "If I was you, I'd probably go crazy with trying to figure out who did in who and why. Maybe you need to step away from the whole thing for a couple of days and the muddy water will clear up a mite."

"Maybe."

She looked straight up into his eyes. "Marshal, you could stay here with me a night or two."

Longarm looked at her with a question in his eyes. "Sleep in the barn?"

"I don't know," she said, banging the ashes from her pipe and moving closer. "We could go back to my cabin, sip a little corn liquor, and talk about something besides Jesse and Buster getting killed."

"You'll want to talk horses and I don't know enough about them to carry on much of a conversation."

"Horses ain't the only things I like."

Annie placed her hands on Longarm's hips. "I get lonesome out here and tired of Tall Tom and satisfying his needs."

"You've got needs of your own."

"I do. Told you I missed not having a husband. Even one as bad as Jethro warmed my bed on cold nights." Annie reached up on her toes and kissed Longarm's mouth. "It's nice to feel a big man."

Longarm tossed his cigar aside and made up his mind to get past the taste of her horse and tobacco smell. Annie Martin was a lonely, healthy young woman and Longarm was tired of having nothing but murders on his mind. Maybe she was right and he needed to step back a day or two and clear his mind and body.

Chapter 17

As they walked back to the cabin, Annie slipped her arm around Longarm's waist, looked up at him, and said, "I ain't the cleanest cowgirl in Arizona, you know."

"You're fine."

"I'd sorta like to take a bath in the water tank I keep out back by the spring. Want to join me?"

Longarm shrugged. It was dark and the spring was up in the trees, but if Annie was going to go to the trouble of washing herself up in preparation for their lovemaking, shouldn't he agree to do the same? He wasn't exactly smelling like a rose either.

"Yeah," he said, "I'll join you."

"We'll get some soap, have us a good splash."

"Sounds like fun," he said, hoping the springwater wasn't going to be too chilly.

Inside the cabin, Annie lit a kerosene lantern and grabbed a bar of soap and a couple of dirty towels. Then they headed up to the spring. The water tank was huge and oak-sided, and must have been used to refill the boilers of railroad steam engines.

"Where'd you get this thing?" Longarm asked.

"My pa and me stole it off the Santa Fe Railroad a few

years back. Had to chop down the tower it was standing on first, then had a hell of a job getting it onto a big wagon."

"I'll bet you did."

"I let folks that want to use it," Annie explained. "It's mostly already filled, but I need to top it off now and then. We'll also have to scoop off the moss and leaves when we climb inside."

"How do we get into that thing?" Longarm asked, staring at the sides, which were at least eight feet tall.

"It's got a ladder on the other side. Shuck out of them clothes, Marshal, and let's see how long you hang!"

Longarm was grateful for the flickering lamplight because Annie had a directness that could be a bit embarrassing. "Ladies first," he said, unbuckling his gunbelt.

Annie didn't even bother to unbutton her shirt, but just pulled it over her head. She wasn't wearing any undergarments, and when Longarm saw the size and shape of her breasts, he felt his pulse quicken with anticipation.

"You must like the looks of what you seen of me so far," Annie said with a bold grin, shaking her torso so that her big breasts jiggled provocatively.

"I do," he admitted, hanging his gunbelt on the branch of a nearby pine, then kicking off his boots and removing his socks.

"Glad to hear that," Annie told him, pulling off her boots and spurs. Once that was done, she tore off her pants. There was nothing under her pants but smooth white skin.

"What do you think of the rest of me?" Annie asked, striking a silly pose and trying not to giggle.

"It all goes together real nice."

"Well, hurry up and come on in!" she told him as she hung the lamp on a peg and climbed the ladder.

Longarm finished undressing and climbed the rungs. He sort of tumbled into the tank, and the water was so cold it took his breath away. "Tarnation!" he shouted, realizing that he couldn't touch the bottom.

"Don't you like to swim, Marshal!" she cried, splashing him with a huge wave composed of leaves and soggy pine needles.

Longarm grabbed her. They both went down poking and pushing all the way to the bottom, then pushed off the floor and burst up through the water's surface.

"Whew!" Annie cried, grabbing the rim of the tank and spitting over the side. "It sure wakes a person up in a hurry!"

Longarm was more than awake . . . he was already aroused. He pinned Annie to the mossy side of the tank and when she tried to duck under his arm, he pulled her very close.

"Where are you hurrying off to?" he asked, noticing how the lamplight was haloing the canopy of leaves overhanging them.

"I was going to get the soap."

"To hell with the soap."

"But . . ."

Longarm kissed her lips and Annie wrapped her arms, then her legs around his waist. It took only a moment for him to find entry into her warm honey pot so that they were joined at the hips.

"Oh," she breathed. "I didn't think you could get it up so big in this cold water . . . but you did. I guess you got me pinned for sure."

"I do," he said, bumping her up a little higher in the tank because she was submerged to her chin. "So what do you think?"

"I believe we could do it a whole lot easier on solid footing."

"I suppose that's true."

"But this is . . . well, different."

He began to move his hips in a slow, pulsating way,

149

and Annie closed her eyes and laid her chin on his shoulder. "Marshal, you're a big, big man."

"And you're a very desirable young woman."

"You think so?"

"I *know* so."

"Jesse was always trying to put it into me, but I never let him do more than suck my nipples."

Longarm wasn't interested in hearing what Jesse or any other man had done to Annie, so he kissed her again and kept kissing her until she gave up trying to talk.

"How's it feel?" he asked.

"I'm sorta feeling . . . well, don't get mad but it's a little hard to do it like this, ain't it?"

"You want to get out and go to the cabin?"

"Maybe not that far. We got a couple of towels." Annie shivered and looked up at the night sky. "The moon is out and the night air is a whole lot warmer than this water tank, don't you think?"

"Yeah, I do," he said, retracting his rod, climbing out of the tank, and navigating his way carefully down the ladder.

Annie was right behind him, and when she spread the towels out beside the water tank and then lay down on her back, Longarm didn't need any urging on what to do next. He pushed her knees apart and buried himself to the hilt in her warm honey pot.

"This is much better," she said, opening herself as wide as she could and moaning with pleasure.

Longarm took his time. The night air combined with the cold water on his back caused him to shiver, and that seemed to excite Annie all the more as their lovemaking became more and more urgent and frenetic.

"Oh," she whispered, "I needed this so bad!"

"So did I."

"I've got a stud horse and whenever he mounts one of my mares, I get all excited and itchy. Can you guess where I need to be rubbed?"

150

"I can guess."

"You're scratchin' that itch right now," Annie said, hugging him tighter and tighter. "But could you do it a little harder?"

Longarm was willing to oblige. He began thrusting powerfully, and Annie quickened the pace of her own surging until they both began to quiver and shout. Annie kept bucking, shoving, and struggling for several moments after Longarm had emptied his seed into her slick little body. But finally, she relaxed and hugged his neck.

"If it was this good out here on the ground, it'll even be better in my bed," she promised.

"I don't see how that could be possible."

Longarm rolled off her and started to say something more, then saw two eyes staring at him from the darkness. He jumped up and lunged for this pistol, figuring it might be Link Dunn or someone intent on putting an end to his murder investigation.

"No!" Annie shouted, tackling him just as he yanked his gun out of its holster and started to fire.

They hit the ground and Longarm's finger involuntarily squeezed off a shot, sending a bullet into the oak tank. A thin but powerful stream of water gushed out from near the bottom of the tank to douse both Custis and Annie.

"Who was that!" Longarm shouted, raising his gun and seeking a target.

"It was my stud horse. Don't kill him, Marshal Long!"

"A horse?"

"Sure. He smelled us doing it and came running. He's a randy old fella and they can tell when some action is going on."

"That's ridiculous!"

"No, it ain't," Annie insisted. "Whenever Tall Tom manages to get between my legs, that old stud horse comes around."

"Well," Longarm said, still not sure if he believed the

young woman or not, "your horse almost got himself shot."

"Glad you didn't because he's a good one," Annie said, frowning at the leak in her water tank. "Gonna have to whittle me a plug. You got a knife handy or do I need to go down to the cabin?"

Longarm carried a pocketknife in his pants, and even opened it for her. Annie tested the sharpness and smiled with satisfaction. "Good knife. Is it a barlow?"

"Yes."

"I had one but lost it."

"You can have mine as a gift."

"Thanks a lot, Marshal."

"I think we're familiar enough with each other that we ought to use our first names."

"Okay, Custis." Annie tore a branch off a tree and quickly whittled a proper plug. She jammed it into the tank's leak and said, "In no time at all, it'll swell up just like that big thing hangin' between your legs and stop the leak. You still leakin' from our lovemaking, Custis?"

"Maybe a little."

"Let's go on down to the cabin and have some more of each other soon as you're able."

"All right," he said, grabbing up his clothes, his gunbelt, and the lantern before leading the way.

When they got back inside the cabin, Longarm used a towel to dry himself off, and then he sat back while Annie poured them both a couple of glasses of corn liquor. "Grab hold of yourself," she warned, " 'cause this is sure to put the lead back in your pencil!"

Annie wasn't fooling. The corn liquor burned all the way down, but then it sort of spread out to warm Longarm's belly. "Where'd you get this stuff?"

"Tall Tom has some friends that make it up in the mountains. I don't ask questions." Annie found her corncob pipe and filled it while she stared at Longarm. "You sure are a handsome man. Why didn't you ever get married?"

"I almost did a few times," he admitted. "But then either the girl or myself changed our minds at the last minute. The truth of the matter is that I travel so much that I'd make a poor husband."

"I don't know that I agree with that," Annie told him. "And besides, you could always quit your job. Custis, are you any good at breaking wild horses?"

"Nope."

"Don't matter," she said, puffing thoughtfully. "My daddy taught me most all there is to know about horses. I'd enjoy teaching you, if you were willing to watch, listen, and learn."

"To tell you the truth, Annie, I'm sort of good at what I do now and I enjoy being a federal marshal."

"But you told me you didn't have any idea who killed Jesse and Buster and you were just sort of worried about the whole thing. It didn't sound to me like you were enjoying trying to catch the murderer."

"This has been an especially difficult case," Longarm confessed. "At first I was afraid Jesse was the guilty party. Then he pretty well convinced me of his innocence, and I accepted that it was Buster who tossed the deadly scorpions on those two poor fellas. But then Buster was murdered, and when Delia married Jesse on his deathbed, that got me to thinking that it had to be either her or Hank Walton."

"Well, they could have done it." Annie took a sip of the corn liquor and her lips drew back. She shook her head, cleared her throat, and added, "I'm not saying that I know for sure that Delia didn't have anything to do with the murders. I just don't think she's that kind any more than Jesse had it in him to be a back-shooter or ambusher."

"The whole thing is a mystery," Longarm admitted.

153

"Maybe the truth is staring me in the face and I just can't see it."

"Maybe," Annie said, "you ought to think about a new line of work. I don't make a lot of money buying, breaking, and selling horses, but the two of us could do pretty well. I've got a nice place, and if we got along as well as I think we would, maybe we could get hitched next year."

"It's tempting and by far the best proposition I've had in quite some time," Longarm said. "But . . ."

"Now don't say no just yet," Annie interrupted. "Let's spend a few days together and let me work my wiles on you and show you how good I can treat a man. By tomorrow night, you could change your mind and never want to leave my bed."

He had to laugh. "I'm not doubting that, if what we did up by the water tank was any indication of what is in store."

"I'm gonna love you like you've never been loved before," Annie told him with a wink of her eye. "Are you ready for another tumble?"

Longarm sipped some corn liquor and decided that he probably would have to wait another ten or fifteen minutes. Even so, he couldn't help but think that the next day or two were going to put this whole miserable murder case in its true perspective.

Chapter 18

Longarm stayed two nights with Annie. He met Tall Tom, a handsome young Yavapai Indian who arrived one afternoon, but departed as soon as he could make a dignified retreat.

"Tall Tom doesn't like white men much," Annie explained after the Indian departed. "So you shouldn't take his unfriendliness personally."

"I didn't."

"You gonna stay around today?"

"I'd like to," he said, meaning it. "But I have to start doing something to figure out who killed Jesse and Buster."

"I'll take you over to the Dunn Ranch," Annie decided. "Maybe if I'm there, Link won't blow up and want to fight."

"I can go alone," Longarm told her. "I don't want you getting crossways with your neighbors on my account."

"Link is already mad at me for not droppin' my pants when he asked."

"For crying out loud! The man has a wife and two kids," Longarm snapped.

"He doesn't care. Link isn't above getting a little on

155

the side wherever he can find it. I really don't like him so I never gave him a tumble."

"Give me directions and I'll go there alone."

"No," Annie insisted. "He'll be better behaved if I'm riding with you. So I'm coming."

Longarm wanted to argue, but then Annie said, "I'm not giving you directions, so quit arguing with me and let's saddle our horses and ride on over there to pay Link and Carol a visit."

It was a two-hour ride over to the Dunn homestead, and when they rode up to the large cabin, the whole family appeared.

"Hello, Marshal. Annie," Carol Dunn said. "Why don't you step down and come inside? I'll make you a cool drink and something to eat."

"We can't stay but a few minutes," Annie said, glancing sideways at Longarm. "We're just out for a ride today."

Carol glanced at her husband, whose lips were drawn in a thin, tight line. Link hadn't said a word yet, but his eyes were unfriendly and it was clear he wasn't pleased by this visit.

"Maybe they don't want to stay," Link finally growled. "Maybe they need to ride on."

"Now, Link," Carol said sharply. "Let's not be unfriendly to our guests."

Longarm decided there was nothing to do but dismount and maybe try to learn a little more about Link Dunn through his wife. It was obvious that the rancher himself wasn't about to do much talking.

"Come on inside," Carol insisted after they tied their horses to a hitching rail. "I was just starting to cook rabbit stew. It'll be ready in only an hour. Won't you stay for supper?"

"No, thanks," Longarm told the woman as they moved into the rambling cabin, which was neat and nicely furnished.

Link took the only man-sized chair in the house. The chair faced a rock fireplace, and the rancher didn't bother to turn it around toward his guests. Longarm had never appreciated being shunned, and it made him feel perverse enough to go over to the fireplace, lean against it, and say, "How is life treating you, Link?"

The big rancher glared up at him, lips pressed together.

Longarm started to enjoy himself. "You have some nice cattle out there, but we saw a couple places where your fences could use some work."

"Is that right?" the rancher grated.

"Yep," Longarm said cheerfully. "And it's too bad about Beaver Creek. Probably going to cost a lot of money to bring water to your lower pastures, huh?"

Link's face darkened and, when he spoke, his voice was thick with anger. "What do you care? You and Jesse were old lawmen friends. I have always judged a man by the company he keeps and your friend was no better than pond scum."

Longarm took the insult with a smile. He gazed over Link's head toward his wife and Annie. They were staring, expressions tense. Longarm glanced back down at Link and said, "Well, I don't much care what you think of me, or Jesse. But someone shot him and I was just wondering if it was you."

Link's eyes widened and he jumped out of his chair to attack. Longarm timed his punch perfectly, and caught the rancher at the point of his jaw with a solid crack that knocked Link back into the chair. Carol cried out in alarm as her husband struggled to rise. Longarm hit him again, this time in the cheek, opening a gash. Link fell back dazed.

"You hurt him!" Carol cried, rushing over. "Leave my house!"

But Longarm shook his head. "I'm not going anywhere until he behaves himself and answers my questions."

Carol ran into the kitchen and hurried back with a wet

towel, which she pressed against her husband's bloody cheek. "What gives you the right to strike him!" she demanded, eyes flashing.

"Better that I walloped him a couple times than be forced to shoot him," Longarm said matter-of-factly. "You husband needs to be taught some manners."

Longarm's voice took on an edge as he turned his attention to the dazed rancher. "Mr. Dunn, I'm an officer of the law and I have two unexplained murders to solve. I rode all the way over here in the performance of my official duties, and you, sir, are going to answer my questions."

Link pushed his wife away and stared at the blood on the towel Carol had pressed against his cheek. He took a deep breath and said, "You had the advantage on me, Marshal. Why don't we step outside and stand toe-to-toe and see what happens?"

"No!" Carol cried.

The rancher heaved a sigh, then said, "What was your question again?"

"Jesse told me that his brother, Buster, was the Scorpion Murderer. Would you agree?"

"Yes. Buster was cut of the same cloth as Jesse, except he was stupid."

"Did you kill either Jesse or Buster up in Flagstaff?"

"No."

"Can you prove it?"

"I was here with Carol and my two sons."

"Where are your boys?"

"Repairing the fence line about a mile east of here."

"I'd like to ask them to back up that you were here," Longarm said. "Any problem with that?"

Link's eyes narrowed. "No, but that better be all that you ask 'em or I'll be hunting you up, Marshal."

"Don't threaten me," Longarm said. "And I'd advise you to learn some better manners."

Link acted like he wanted to climb out of the chair

158

again, but when Longarm clenched his big fists, the rancher wisely decided to let the warning pass.

"Annie, let's go talk to the boys," said Longarm.

Annie took a deep breath and said to Carol, "I'm sorry about this, but Marshal Long is up against it in this murder business."

"Both my husband and I hated Jesse Jerome, but we didn't have anything to do with killing the man or his brother."

"I believe you," Annie said, glancing at Link and then saying to Longarm, "Let's ride out to see Todd and Jeff."

If Link Dunn had been packing a pistol, Longarm wouldn't have dared to turn his back on the dangerous, hateful rancher. But Link was unarmed, so Longarm went outside, climbed on his horse, and rode off with Annie.

"You were awfully hard on Link," Annie said when they had ridden about a mile.

"Remember what you told me about outlaws? The kind that will never be broke and can never be trusted?"

"Yes."

"Link is like that," Longarm said. "Somewhere in his past he's killed men before. Maybe in the war, maybe Indians, or maybe he committed murder. It doesn't matter. Link would take a man's life without giving it a second thought."

"Like Jesse Jerome?"

"Yeah," Longarm said reluctantly.

"But not like you," Annie told him. "You've killed men but you remember every one of them, don't you."

"They all bothered me," Longarm admitted. "Even the worst of them. But I don't want to talk about me. I want to talk to the Dunn kids."

"They're good boys. Open and friendly like their mother."

Longarm and Annie soon found the Dunn boys, and Longarm doubted that either one of them was still in his teens. They were tall, skinny, and tough-looking kids.

159

When they saw Annie and Longarm, they stopped working and waited for the riders to state their business.

"Hi, boys," Annie said. "This is Marshal Custis Long."

They nodded to Longarm, eyes frank and appraising. Not friendly, but not unfriendly either.

"Which one are you?" Longarm asked, pointing to the older one.

"Jeff. Jeff Dunn."

"Jeff, I want you to come over here so we can talk for a moment in private."

Jeff looked to Annie, who smiled and nodded. The boy followed Longarm's horse off a little ways. Longarm didn't dismount, but instead pushed his hat back and leaned forward on his saddle horn. "Jeff, I need to know what you have been up to the last three or four days."

"Workin', same as we always do."

"With your brother?"

"And my pa. We been digging an irrigation ditch to bring water down to the lower pastures."

"I see." Longarm straightened. "So your father has been here every day the last week?"

"Yes, sir. We ain't got the money to hire work out. Got to dig that ditch by ourselves. Sometimes Mom even helps, but Pa don't let her do it for long 'cause the dirt is hard with rocks."

"Okay," Longarm said, satisfied with the answer. "Ask your brother to come over here for a minute."

"Yes, sir. Is something wrong?"

"I hit your father a couple of times in the face, but he'll be all right."

Jeff's eyes widened. "And he didn't shoot you?"

Longarm almost smiled. "I think he wanted to, but I didn't give him the chance."

Jeff shook his head. "You were real lucky he didn't kill you."

"He's killed men before, hasn't he." It wasn't a question.

160

"Pa fought for the Union as a captain in the cavalry. So, yes, sir, he killed a few Johnny Rebs. But he lost his own pa and all five of his brothers in the war. He don't like to talk about it much and we don't ask questions."

"Let me speak to Todd."

The younger brother came over, and Longarm asked the kid the same questions and received the same answers.

"Okay, Todd. Don't work too hard because you're still kind of young."

"I'm near a man," Todd said, raising up on his toes. "And maybe I'd like to be a lawman myself some day."

"You have a long time yet to decide. Listen, Todd. I told your brother that I hit your pa a couple of times."

"You *hit* him?"

"Yeah."

"And he didn't whip or kill you?"

"No."

"Why not?"

"Doesn't matter. The point is that I thought he might have killed Mr. Jerome and a fella named Buster."

"I knew 'em both. Buster was crazy. He liked snakes and stuff like that."

"Did you ever see him with scorpions?"

"Yes, sir." Todd looked down at the earth and toed it for a moment before saying, "You're wondering if he killed the governor and the reporter with them scorpions, ain't you?"

"Yes."

"I'm sure he did it. But Pa wouldn't kill a man like that. He'd face 'em up and shoot 'em down."

"I believe you," Longarm said. "Do you know anyone else that might have shot Mr. Jerome?"

"Lots of people wanted to do it. I'm glad he's dead. Maybe now we can get Beaver Creek back and won't have to spend all our time diggin' a ditch."

Longarm motioned for Annie to join him. He waved good-bye to the Dunn boys and he and Annie rode away.

"Well, did you get the answers you wanted?"

"I didn't want any particular answer," Longarm told her. "All I wanted was the truth."

"Are you satisfied that Link isn't the killer?"

"Yes. And I'm satisfied that Buster was the Scorpion Murderer."

"So who is next on your list of suspects?" Annie asked. "Am I a suspect?"

"Do you got an alibi?"

"You could talk to Tall Tom," she suggested. "He'd tell you that I've been around except for this last trip to Prescott to get the supplies and grain you helped me unload."

Longarm shook his head. "You didn't kill Jesse or Buster."

"Then who did?"

"Maybe Delia."

"I don't think so," Annie said, shaking her head. "I think you'd better get back to Agate and start asking questions."

"I will, and I guess we might as well split up right now."

"You're welcome back when you've solved the murders," Annie said, looking him in the eye. "My offer stands."

"Thanks, Annie."

Longarm would have liked to give the woman a hug, but instead he just tipped his hat to Annie and rode toward Agate wondering if Jesse's killer was someone he still hadn't even met.

Chapter 19

When Longarm rode back into Agate, he could almost feel the change in the town's mood. Now that Jesse was dead and Delia had made her plans to resurrect the town well known, people looked a lot happier. He saw men shake hands and he heard laughter. The atmosphere had changed completely.

The first thing Longarm did was to ride up to Jesse's mansion and tie his horse at the hitching rail. The mansion was a big Victorian place with a white picket fence protecting rose gardens, and when Longarm knocked on the door, a formal-looking man in his sixties appeared.

"I'm Marshal Custis Long. Is Mrs. Ballou here?"

"No, sir, but Mrs. Jerome is at home. Would you like me to ask if she'll see you?"

"Yes."

"Please wait on the porch, Marshal."

The man shut the door, and Longarm took a seat on a porch swing. From this vantage point, he could look out over the town and beyond to the surrounding mountains. It was a fine view, and a soft breeze made the late afternoon pleasant.

"Custis!" Delia called, coming out to join him on the swing. "You look tired and trail-worn."

"I've been out hunting for answers," he said, thinking that Delia was the happiest-looking widow he'd ever seen and also the most attractive.

"Did you find any?"

"No," he admitted. "Well, that's not entirely true. I've eliminated Link Dunn from my short list of murder suspects."

"I never believed he ought to be a suspect in the first place," she said. "I think you need to rest a day or two, then return to Flagstaff and question Mike Kelly."

"I may have to do that," Longarm agreed. "You sure look pretty for being a woman in mourning."

Delia actually blushed. "You know that I didn't love Jesse. And I know that people are saying what I did was scandalous. But you see, I did it for Agate. I married Jesse because it was the one way that I could undo all the harm he'd done to this town. And I'm going to help build it back to what it once was, only even better."

"That's admirable."

"I feel lucky to have the opportunity. But that doesn't help you solve the mystery of Jesse's murder, does it."

"No. Nor that of his brother, Buster."

"I don't know what to tell you, Custis. Perhaps you should let it all pass."

"You mean just go away and let whoever killed them get off scot-free?"

Delia looked away. "Whoever killed Jesse and Buster did everyone in Agate a big, big favor. I'm not saying that I condone murder or that I'm happy that Jesse was shot and killed . . . but much good did come from their deaths and whoever is responsible would be considered a hero in this town."

"Did you kill Jesse?"

Delia threw back her head and laughed.

"All right," Longarm said, regretting the question, "then

164

why don't you at least give me your list of suspects."

"I don't have a list," she replied. "I'm far more concerned with the future than the past. I've got a lot of good work to do here. Dwelling on Jesse's death would be a waste of time and entirely counterproductive."

"I see." Longarm removed his hat and laid it on his lap. He gazed out at the town and rocked back and forth in the swing for a few moments before saying, "You may not be interested in finding the murderer, but it's my job. And I don't consider solving two murders a waste of time or being counterproductive."

"I didn't mean that you should."

"Delia, I need your help. I'm not going back to Denver without finding the killer and bringing him or her to justice."

"Her?"

"It could be a woman."

"Like me, or Carol or Annie?" Delia's eyebrows shot up. "Custis, be serious!"

"Someone gunned down Buster at the cabin. And whoever shot Jesse was a pretty good marksman. The light was poor and it wouldn't have been an easy shot."

"Well, I'm a terrible shot," Delia said. "And I'm sure that Carol isn't much better. Annie . . . well, she's half man, so I suppose she's good with weapons, but I can't say for sure."

"What about Hank?"

"Hank?" Delia's eyes widened. "Hank Walton wouldn't hurt a fly! He and my late husband were the very best of friends. They shared an interest in art, music, and wood carving. No, Custis, Hank isn't your killer."

"Hank is in love with you, isn't he?"

Delia took a deep breath. "There's no point in denying the fact. Yes, Hank loves and wants to marry me."

"And what do you think about that?"

"I'm a widow in mourning. Or at least, a widow. I may well marry Hank when enough time has passed."

"Then he'd stand to gain a lot."

Delia's expression changed and her eyes narrowed. "That's a terrible thing to say."

"Why? It's the truth."

"I think you ought to go now before I get angry and we have hard words."

"All right, but first give me a few possibilities as to who might have killed Jesse and his brother."

"You could go to any merchant on Main Street—those that are still in business—and they would tell you they hated Jesse. But did one of them kill him or Buster? I have no earthly idea."

"All right," Longarm said, coming to his feet. "I'll just keep asking questions. Sooner or later someone will say something that will lead me to the murderer."

"I still say you ought to let it go," Delia told him, coming to her feet. "You were sent out to find the Scorpion Murderer and you've done that. So you really haven't failed. We have a local deputy who runs the jail. Why don't you throw it in his lap and go back to Denver?"

"Because your deputy is just a part-time jail guard who occasionally ventures out into the street half afraid of his own shadow. He's not a lawman and never could be."

"We're going to hire a professional when this town gets back on its feet," Delia promised. "We're going to make Agate a law-abiding town where people feel safe and where local ordinances are enforced."

"I think that's a fine idea," Longarm told her as he replaced his hat and headed back to town.

Longarm headed for the Ponderosa Cafe to see Hank Walton. The place was closed up, but when he peered in the window, he saw the cafe owner and another woman back in the kitchen. Longarm couldn't hear what they were saying, but he could see that they were having a violent argument. Curious as to what was going on, he stepped around the building and walked up to the back

166

door of the cafe. Putting his ear to the door, he again tried to overhear the conversation.

The door was thick and solid so he couldn't make out the words, but it was plain that Walton and the woman were both incensed. Longarm moved back down the alley and stepped in between a pair of buildings. If he heard screams, he would come to the woman's rescue; if not, he would try to find out who she was and why she was so upset with Hank Walton.

The back door of the Ponderosa Cafe flew open and Longarm saw the woman come flying out to crash and roll over twice in the dirt.

"Damn you!" she screamed at Walton, who stood in the doorway wearing his apron. "You may think that you got rid of me and the children, but you haven't! How can you do this to us and live with yourself?"

"If I ever see you in this town again, I'll make you wish you were never born!" Walton bellowed. "And don't you *ever* come to see me again!"

The woman found a rock, jumped up, and hurled it at the cafe owner, who wisely slammed the door just before he would have been beaned. She buried her face in her hands and began to sob hysterically.

The woman finally fell silent, then drew herself up and brushed off her dress. The alley was in shadows, but Longarm could see that she was a short, dumpy lady wearing a shapeless housedress. For the first time, he noticed that she had a little cardboard suitcase, which she now collected before leaving to shuffle down the alley still crying softly.

Longarm followed her to the main street. He watched as the woman, now plainly visible, again dusted herself off. She also drew out a handkerchief and blew her nose. Her face was red, and she gazed forlornly up and down the street as if she had no idea of what to do or where to go next.

"Excuse me," Longarm said, hurrying over to the

woman. "I'm United States Marshal Custis Long and I can see that you're upset. Is there something I can do to help you, ma'am?"

She looked up at him, a very plain woman probably old before her time with a wart on her right cheek and red, puffy eyes. "Thank you, Marshal, but I'll be all right."

"Are you sure?"

"When is the next stage to Prescott?"

"I'm not certain, but we could walk down to the stage office and find out."

"Yes," she said, "I'd better do that."

"Let me help you," he said, reaching for her battered little suitcase.

She gave him a fleeting look of appreciation, and they began to walk along together. Longarm could hear her sniffle. Her head was downcast and her hair was a tangle of brown streaked with gray. Compared to Delia, she was a pitiful and sorry sight.

"What's your name?" he asked.

"Alice."

"Alice, uh . . ."

"Alice . . . Smith."

"I see. Well, Mrs. Smith, what brings you to Agate?"

"I . . . I came to see someone."

"And who would that be?" he asked innocently.

She started to answer. Then her step faltered and she covered her face and began to weep. Longarm eased her out of the foot traffic and between two buildings, then put his arm around her shoulders. "Mrs. Smith," he said gently, "I'm a lawman and I can read faces and voices pretty well. I have to in order to do my job. It's obvious that you're very upset and in trouble. Why don't you let me help you?"

She stopped crying and lustily blew her nose. Alice, or whatever her name was, looked devastated. "Marshal," she began, "I *am* in trouble. I'm a married woman whose husband abandoned me and my two children down in Tucson about three years ago. I've found my husband, but he wants nothing to do with me or the kids anymore and we desperately need his help."

Longarm spied a bench under a big tree where two old men were sitting and talking. He led Alice over to the bench and said, "Gentlemen, we need some privacy here. Will you excuse us?"

"Huh?" one of them asked.

"Move along for a few minutes," Longarm told them with a trace of steel in his voice.

The pair got up and shuffled away, but not before they gave him a couple of scowls.

"Sit down and rest your feet, Mrs. Smith," he said.

"Don't call me that. I hate deception. My real name is Mrs. Beesley. Alice Beesley from Tucson. My children are Sarah and George. They're just seven and five years old and they've almost never seen their father."

"Who is he?"

Alice looked at him and fresh tears filled her eyes. "I'm afraid to tell you, Marshal."

"I can't help you if you won't help me," he said. "Come on now, Mrs. Beesley. Who is your husband?"

"Hank . . . Walton."

Longarm had already guessed as much, and he wondered if Delia had any idea that her good and kind "gentleman" friend was really a louse, a cad, and a liar.

"I know Hank."

"He says that he's going to marry a woman named Delia Jerome. I've heard all about her. She's a rich lady now, isn't she?"

"Yes."

"A widow who married some wealthy man on his deathbed for his money?"

"That's about the size of it."

"Is she also . . . pretty?"

Longarm hated to answer the question. "Yes, she is."

"Then no wonder Hank doesn't want anyone to know that he has a wife and two young children! I don't suppose he told anyone that he's spent time in prison either."

"Prison?"

"He killed a man in a gunfight soon after we were married. He claimed it was self-defense. You see, my husband was quite a drinker and gambler. He was also a thief and a wife-beater, though I didn't know any of those things when we were married ten years ago. And when he killed that man in a gunfight, I stood up for him and begged the judge to be lenient. I'm sure that's why Hank only got two years in the Yuma Penitentiary."

"That's not much time for a killing."

"I told the judge that Hank was a good man and husband. I lied, but I thought I was doing what was best for us all."

"But that was a mistake."

"Yes," Alice said. "When Hank was released, he only came to see me once, and that was for . . . well, what he wanted was to use me for pleasure and then to take whatever money I had saved. I gave him the first, of course, it being my wifely duty. But when he realized I only had forty dollars saved, he beat me real bad and ran off. I ain't never seen him until this very day."

"Hank can't do that to a wife and his children," Longarm said, not sure of the law in such a case, but convinced that Hank could be brought back to court and ordered to at least support his two children.

"Hank swears that if he marries the Jerome widow, he'll be rich and then he'll send me money. I told him that I couldn't wait. My children are near destitute, Marshal! We been waiting and hoping for years that Hank would come back and help us, but I can see now that he has no intention of doing that!"

"We'll go talk to him again," Longarm said, getting

angrier by the moment. "And you can be sure that I'll tell Delia about his past."

"No! Hank swore he'd kill me if word got to her about his still being married with kids. He says that if I get a divorce down in Tucson, he'll send me a thousand dollars."

"And you believed him?" Longarm asked in amazement.

"What else can I do?"

Longarm considered the poor woman's dilemma for several moments, then said, "I have a hunch that Hank is in more trouble than you can imagine."

"Did he kill someone else?"

"I think so," Longarm told her. "But I can't be sure. If I can prove it, then he'll go to prison and this time it would be for life."

"That wouldn't help me or my children!"

"Yes, it would," Longarm said. "Hank must own a house."

"He does! I asked the first person I met when I arrived where he lived and they gave me directions. He's got a nice house on the next street over. We never had a house of our own. We rent a shack down in Tucson in the poorest part of town and—"

"How would you like to own that house and his cafe to boot?" Longarm interrupted.

Her jaw dropped. Then she recovered and asked, "But how could—"

"If he's guilty of murder and you are still married, you would get what he owns."

"Are you sure?"

"Yes," Longarm said, this time without hesitation. "Hank would go before a judge who would sentence him to life in prison. You and your children would simply have the house and the property as his next of kin."

Her calloused hand flew to her mouth. "Oh, my goodness! But if he ever got out, he would come back here and kill me!"

"I give you my word that he won't ever see the light of freedom again. Not after all the things that you've told me and what I suspect he's done while living here in Agate."

"Marshal," she said, taking his hands in her own. "I'm really scared. I'm not a brave woman and if he did kill me, who'd take care of my two orphaned children? Hank wouldn't. He won't even claim them now."

"Mrs. Beesley. Your husband is a dangerous and clever man who has pulled the wool over everyone's eyes. I need you to help me prove that he killed two men, Jesse Jerome and Buster Jerome. If you agree to help, then I swear I'll protect you and see that you are rewarded with your husband's house and cafe."

"I'm a very good cook," she told him, looking away and sniffling a few times. "I always dreamed of having a cafe. I taught Hank how to cook."

"Help me out," Longarm said, almost pleading.

She bit her lip. "I'm so afraid. More for my children than for myself. I left 'em in Tucson, but I have to go back soon. I was hoping that Hank would come home and stay with us, but he won't. He's a terrible man, Marshal. I'm sorry I ever fell in love with him, but he fooled me good."

"Don't feel so bad. Will you help me?"

"I . . . don't know."

"If you don't, I can't arrest your husband and you'll go back to Tucson with nothing. If I can pin the murders on him, he'll go to prison for life and you'll be able to bring your children up to Agate. To a house and a business that you own. So which is it going to be, Alice?"

She began to tremble, and just when he thought she was going to say no, the woman blurted out, "If Hank kills me, you got to promise to take care of my kids until they're grown. Will you promise to do that?"

"I promise."

"Swear to the Lord?"

"Yes."

"All right then, what do you want me to do?"

Longarm thought about it for a moment. He'd only get Alice to help him one time. If anything went wrong, she'd be so frightened that she'd never have the nerve to help a second time . . . if she was still alive.

"See that hotel up the street?"

"The Agate Hotel?"

"That's right. I want you to get a room there and stay put for a while."

She took a deep breath. "How much would such a nice hotel cost?"

He read her mind and gave her ten dollars. "Find something to eat . . . not at the Ponderosa Cafe, of course. Then go get a room. Register as Mrs. Beesley and stay put until I show up either this evening or tomorrow morning. Will you do that?"

"I'm scared!"

"I'm also staying there and I'll be close if your husband should appear. You have to help me. Can you do it?"

"Yes."

"All right then," Longarm told her. "Just go along and be brave and everything will work out fine."

Alice Beesley stood up and brushed the loose tendrils of hair from her not very pretty face. She nodded and reached to touch Longarm's cheek. "You just remember your promise about my children. My life isn't worth much of anything now, but theirs is just beginning and they're fine children."

"I'll remember my promise, but you're going to be just fine."

"I'll go eat. I haven't had much to eat lately. I barely had the fare to get me a round-trip ticket. I'm near faint with hunger."

"Eat and go get a room. Then rest and wait for me to

173

knock on your door, but keep it bolted and don't let anyone but me inside."

"I sure won't, Marshal."

He gave her the little suitcase and watched the poor woman trudge down the street. Men tipped their hats and she managed to smile.

She ain't much to look at, but I like her and I'll bet she has a couple of fine children, Longarm thought to himself as he headed back up the street to see Delia at the mansion.

Chapter 20

Longarm asked to see Delia again, and when she came to the front door of the mansion he said, "I need your help right now."

Delia stepped outside, her expression showing immediate concern. "Are you all right?"

"Yes." He took her arm and led her over to the porch swing, then sat her down and said, "I know that Hank is a good friend of yours and what I have to say is going to come as quite a shock."

"Listen," she began in a stern voice, "I told you that—"

"His name isn't Hank Walton. It's Hank *Beesley*. He's been in the Yuma Prison for murder and he's abandoned a wife and two little children down in Tucson."

"That's preposterous!"

"Who is watching your hotel desk?"

"Why, Mr. Graves. He's retired and really needs the money, but I don't see what that has to do with anything."

"Mr. Graves is just about to register a Mrs. Alice Beesley, who has just arrived nearly penniless from Tucson to plead with her husband, Hank, to help her feed and take care of their two children."

Delia shook her head. "Perhaps she's lying. I can't believe—"

"You'll believe her when you talk to the poor woman," Longarm said. "That's all that I'm asking. Just hear her story and then make up your own mind. Delia, the woman is scared to death that Hank will kill her if she uncovers his true identity."

Delia stood up and expelled a deep breath. "All right. I think this woman is probably a charlatan, but I'll hear her out."

"Good. It's almost dark. We can't afford to see Hank on our way over there or he might get suspicious and run."

"Don't be silly! He has a house, a cafe, and a good reputation in Agate."

"Believe me," Longarm vowed, "that's about to suddenly change."

They waited about thirty minutes and then, satisfied that it was dark enough outside and that Alice would be finished with her meal and registering at the Agate Hotel, Longarm said, "Let's go."

It wasn't a long walk down the hill to the hotel and when they arrived, Longarm stood aside as Delia went up to the dignified old man behind her registration desk and said, "Mr. Graves, did we just receive a new guest?"

"Yes, ma'am. A Mrs. Beesley. She seems to be rather upset and in quite dire circumstances, so I gave her a room for just one dollar."

"Which room?"

"Upstairs, Room 204."

"Perfect," Longarm said because his was the very next room.

"Is something wrong?" the old man asked, looking worried.

"Not yet."

"She seemed respectable enough. I thought that . . ."

"You did just fine," Longarm assured the old man as

he took Delia's arm and they hurried upstairs. When they knocked on the room door, Alice cried, "Who is it!"

"Marshal Custis Long. You can open up, Mrs. Beesley."

The door opened slowly and the poor woman let them in. "Who is she?" Mrs. Beesley asked.

"Mrs. Jerome, this is Mrs. Alice Beesley. I think you two ought to have a little talk while I go next door to my own room and clean up a bit."

"Don't leave!" Alice cried.

"I'll be right next door," Longarm promised her. "Delia, lock the door and don't let anyone in but me."

Delia was staring at Alice so intently that Longarm repeated his request.

"All right," she said absently. "We'll be fine."

Longarm went next door and poured a washbasin full of water from a large porcelain pitcher. He smelled of horse and . . . well, of lusty Annie Martin. He removed his dusty shirt and washed his face, then found his straight razor and soap. He shaved, wondering exactly what was being said next door. That task finished, he yanked off his dirty clothes, cleaning himself up a bit with the fresh water and the washrag. Finally, he dipped his head in the soapy basin water and washed his hair with a piece of soap he carried in his bags.

What I really need is a good soak in a hot bath, he thought. *But that can wait a little longer.*

Longarm changed into clean underwear, pants, and shirt. He buffed his boots with one of his dirty socks and buckled on his gunbelt. Standing in front of a small mirror, he inspected himself, and decided that he now appeared far more respectable and professional. He'd looked so grubby before that it was small wonder Alice Beesley had been so wary and unsure of his abilities.

Feeling cleaner and confident that he could wrap this murder case up tonight with a little help and luck, Longarm stretched out on his bed and made his plans. However, it wasn't five minutes later that he dozed off into a dreamless sleep.

He couldn't have slept more than fifteen minutes when there was a loud knock at his door and he heard Delia call, "Custis, open up!"

Longarm knuckled the sleep from his eyes and opened the door. The two women hurried inside, and when Longarm looked at their faces, he knew that Delia no longer harbored any doubt as to the truth of Alice's plight or of Hank's true identity.

"Alice and I are in this with you all the way," Delia said, laying her arm across the smaller woman's shoulders. "What do you want us to do?"

Longarm motioned the two women to sit on his bed. He took a chair and said, "We need to have Alice get Hank to admit that he murdered both Jesse and Buster."

"I can't do that!"

"Yes, you can and you must," Longarm insisted. "It's the only way we are going to get your deadbeat husband to go to prison for life . . . if not to the gallows."

Alice grew pale, and Longarm guessed the poor, frightened woman would have burst into fresh tears if Delia hadn't put her arm around her and whispered, "Honey, it's going to be all right. The marshal and I will be right next door."

"Alice," Longarm said. "Here is what you have to do and say. First, we'll send a message to the Ponderosa Cafe. You'll write and say that you have decided to stay the night. That you have already talked to me, the federal marshal, and that in the morning, you are also going to tell Mrs. Delia Jerome who he really is."

"But he'll go crazy! He'd do anything to stop me from—"

"Of course he will," Longarm agreed. "Hank will come rushing over here and pound on your door. But he'll have to pass Mr. Graves downstairs at the desk, so he won't

178

be able to do you any harm in your room because everyone would know he was the guilty party."

"But he might go insane and—"

"Alice," Longarm said firmly, "you have to say something like, 'The marshal already knows that you murdered Jesse Jerome and his brother, and when I tell him you already went to prison for murdering a man, he'll probably arrest you for sure.' "

The woman from Tucson began to tremble. "If I tell him that, he might pull out a gun or a knife and kill me on the spot!"

"We'll be right next door listening to every word. When you tell Hank that I suspect him of the killings, he needs to say that he really did do them so that we have the evidence we need to send him to prison or the gallows."

"But how can I do that?"

"You'll figure a way," Longarm said, sounding far more confident than he felt. "Otherwise, I'll only be able to arrest him on lesser charges."

Delia jumped to her feet, looking outraged. "Like beating or knifing poor Alice before we can get into her room and save her life!"

"And for child abandonment," Longarm said, knowing how lame that sounded. "That's why Hank needs to be so furious that he admits to the murders."

"It's too risky!" Delia protested.

"It's her only hope of putting her husband away forever," Longarm said. "And Delia, you will be the witness."

"But what if we can't even hear the confession! The hotel room walls aren't that thin."

"We'll knock a hole in the wall and hang a picture over it so that we can hear perfectly."

Delia shook her head. "Did it take you long to figure out this great scheme?"

"I've done it before a time or two. When a man gets

crazy mad, he'll generally say whatever comes to his mind. Then I've got his confession, and having a witness seals his fate."

Alice was bent over, hands clasped in her lap, rocking slightly back and forth. Delia sat down beside her and whispered, "If you can't go through with this, tell Marshal Long and we'll think of some other way to get Hank to confess."

"Delia, there is no other way," Longarm snapped. "Trust me, this can and will work! Alice, what do you say?"

She raised her head. "I . . . I don't know."

"Think of your children. Think of how little Sarah and George will finally have the home that they deserve and you will at last have a cafe where you can cook good meals and earn an honest and respectable living. Think of your children, Alice!"

She moaned, then took a deep breath. Raising her head, she looked at Custis and said, "All right. I'll do my best."

Longarm wanted to jump forward, grab the poor woman, and kiss her, but instead he nodded with satisfaction. "All right then. Delia, go downstairs and get a paper and pen. And a saw, hammer, and nail or picture hook. While Alice writes the note to be delivered to Hank, I'll cut a foot-square hole in the wall and hang a picture over the hole in Alice's room."

"It's going to make a mess," Delia warned.

"Then you'll need to clean it up before we send the note down to the Ponderosa Cafe."

Delia gave him a hard look, but she hurried downstairs. In less than five minutes, she returned with the writing and carpentry materials that were needed.

"All right," Longarm said. "Alice, write the note just as I tell you."

Longarm slowly dictated the note telling Hank what he needed to know so that he'd have no choice but to come up to Alice's room with the intention of taking her away

180

and killing her where his murderous act would go unseen. The note was short, and Longarm had no doubt it would serve its purpose.

"Who will deliver it?" Delia asked.

"You figure that one out. Go downstairs and into the street. Find someone that looks reliable—maybe a kid—and pay him a dollar to deliver the note to Hank."

"Custis, first you knock a hole in my wall that will cost plenty to fix, and now you want me to—"

"Delia, you are a rich woman!" Longarm snapped. "Now just do it."

"And what do I do?" Alice asked.

"We go to your room, hang a picture over the hole I'm just about to make, and then you wait for Hank to appear. He'll be furious, but let him in anyway. Try to stay away from him, and do whatever it takes to get him to admit murdering Jesse and Buster Jerome."

"And if he tries to kill me?"

"He won't dare fire a gun knowing that Mr. Graves would hear the shot. If he pulls a knife or tries to strangle you, all you have to do is cry out for help and I'll be in this room in less than five seconds."

Alice nodded with understanding. She looked terrified, but that was all right because Hank would expect her to look that way.

They changed rooms. Longarm quickly cut the hole in the wall, making it even larger than a foot square because he'd found a good-sized framed print to cover the larger hole. He and Alice cleaned up the sawdust and mess, then hung the print over the hole. The entire operation took only a couple of minutes.

"I'm so afraid," Alice Beesley repeated.

"It will be over very quickly," Longarm reminded the woman. "Just get him to admit the murders, and your entire life and that of your children will be forever changed for the better."

She bit her lower lip and nodded. Longarm shut her

door and went next door to his own room. Moments later, Delia rushed upstairs and said, "I found a boy just like you suggested. Jimmy Cook will deliver the note without fail. How long do you think it will be before Hank comes rushing up to see Alice?"

"It might take a little while. He'll have to get rid of his customers, and that will take at least a half hour. Then he'll need to lock up before he comes storming over to the hotel."

Longarm went over to the open hole in his wall. He pushed his hand through and nudged the picture aside so that he could look into her room. "Alice?"

She screamed and jumped a foot. "Alice, it's just me. I wanted to say that it might take an hour for Hank to run his customers out of his cafe and get up here. So just try and relax."

"I feel like I'm going to throw up!"

"Try to calm yourself."

"I've been praying. I wish I had the Holy Bible."

"I'll get her a Bible from downstairs, poor thing," Delia said, jumping up and leaving the room on the run.

Longarm figured he had better not interfere. Alice needed to have some semblance of sanity to pull this off, and reading the Bible sure couldn't hurt.

With the picture still pushed aside so that he could see through into Alice's room, Longarm spent the next few minutes trying to reassure the woman that she was going to do fine. Delia had a key and unlocked Alice's room, gave her the Bible and a big hug, then came back to join Longarm.

"On the one hand I hope this takes forever; on the other," Delia breathed, "it must feel like slow death to poor Alice, so I hope that murdering rat comes up soon!"

"Me too," Longarm said, his head still in the hole as he watched Alice, now clutching the Bible in her white-knuckled hands.

Chapter 21

"Here he comes!" Delia whispered, peering through a crack in the curtains. "Hank is practically running! He didn't even take his apron off. Oh, now he did. He threw it away. Custis, I can see his face in the light of the street-lamp and he looks crazy."

"He *is* crazy," Longarm said. "There isn't a gun or a weapon in his hand, is there?"

"Not that I can see."

Longarm reached through the wall and pushed the picture aside slightly. "Alice, Hank is on his way. When he knocks, unlock your door, then step over near this picture but don't touch it. Then tell him what I told you about me knowing he killed Jesse and Buster. Then shut up and let's hear what he says. If he doesn't confess right away, push him a little."

"All right," she wheezed.

"We'll be right here listening and ready to come to your rescue."

"I know."

A few minutes later, they heard the knock on Alice's hotel room door.

"Who is it?"

"You know damn good and well who it is, Alice! Open up!"

"Not if you're going to hurt me."

Good, Longarm thought.

"I . . . I won't hurt you."

"Promise?"

"Yes, gawdammit!"

Alice opened the door, then retreated over near the picture. Longarm had let it slip back into place on her wall, but he could feel her standing just inches from his hands.

"What do you want!"

"I want money, Hank. Money or I'll go and talk to Mrs. Delia Jerome and tell her who you really are!"

That's a girl! You're doing just fine!

"Did you actually tell the marshal that I'd killed a man and gone to prison?"

"Yes."

Longarm heard two jolting steps and then the sound of flesh striking flesh. Delia started to run for the door, but Longarm grabbed and covered her mouth. "Shhh!" he hissed. "We need the confession!"

They both heard Alice start to cry. Then she found the strength and courage to say, "You did kill them! Just like you killed that man down in Tucson!"

"Yeah," Hank snarled, "I killed them! And I'm going to marry Delia and you're not going to mess this up for me!"

"Hank, please don't hit me again!"

"I won't," they heard him say in a suddenly soft and ingratiating voice that sent chills up Longarm's spine. "Alice, we're going to go for a walk and work this out together. When I marry Delia, I can send you and the children money. More money than you'd ever had before. But we need to work it out."

"We can talk here."

"No," Hank said, "someone might—"

Suddenly, the worst imaginable thing happened. Alice

184

must have retreated up against the wall and jolted the picture, because it fell off the nail that Longarm had pounded in the wall.

Hank shouted, "What the . . ."

Longarm drew his six-gun just as the man pushed his face into the hole and stared through the wall. For an instant, they were staring eyeball to eyeball, and then Hank was reaching for his gun. Or at least that was what Longarm had to assume as he rammed his own Colt and fist through the hole and opened fire.

He shot Hank three times at point-blank range, twice in the face. He heard Alice scream and Hank's body strike, then slide down the wall behind him to the floor. By then, Delia was already flying into Alice's room.

Longarm pulled his gun back through the wall, then leaned his forehead against it and closed his eyes.

That was close. Way too damned close, he thought, expelling a deep sigh of relief. *But it worked, and now Alice and her children are going to have a nice new home right here in the resurrected town of Agate, Arizona.*

Watch for

LONGARM AND THE SIX-GUN SENORITA

272nd novel in the exciting LONGARM series
from Jove

Coming in July!

LONGARM

Explore the exciting Old West with one of the men who made it wild!
